Also by Scarlett St. Clair

When Stars Come Out

HADES X PERSEPHONE
A Touch of Darkness
A Touch of Ruin
A Touch of Malice

HADES SAGA
A Game of Fate
A Game of Retribution

ADRIAN X ISOLDE
King of Battle and Blood
Queen of Myth and Monsters

MOUNTAINS
MADE OF
GLASS

A
FAIRYTALE
RETELLING

SCARLETT ST. CLAIR

Published by Bloom Books, an imprint of Sourcebooks
P.O. Box 4410, Naperville, Illinois 60567-4410
(630) 961-3900
sourcebooks.com

Printed and bound in the United States of America.
VP 10 9 8 7 6 5 4 3

For the fuck of it.

Glossary

This glossary serves to offer insight into the origin of the creatures and entities in *Mountains Made of Glass*.

Crone/Witch: In fairytales, a crone or a witch is often an old woman. She can have evil intentions, but I find she can take on a more ambiguous role. She sometimes curses or gives tasks to the hero, who then must overcome the obstacle by demonstrating their morality. She is usually the catalyst to the hero's change, which makes her a very powerful creature in stories.

Red Caps: A type of goblin. In MMOG, these goblins are called red caps because they soak their hats in the blood of their victims. However, in other fairy tales, they are called red caps only because their hats are red. There are variations of redcaps depending on the origin of the fairytale and not all are malevolent.

Sprite: A type of fairy. Sprites are very tiny and are usually attracted to water. They are temperamental and can inflict madness upon a person.

Pixie: A type of fairy. Pixies can be household fairies and are sometimes described as mischievous. They often like to play tricks.

Brownie: Brownies are described as spirits, often those of a dead relative. They are sometimes classified as fairies or hobgoblins, which is why I used them in this retelling. They are usually male, but there are a few females, and they are said to keep house.

Magic Mirror: A reference to the story of Snow White. In particular, it is said that the tale was based on a real person, Maria Sophia Margaretha Catharina von Erthal, who resided near a glass-making region. It was said that the mirrors they made were of such "extraordinary quality, with the glass being of such excellence that people said the mirrors 'always spoke the truth.'"

Elves: A type of fae. I used two types of elves in this story: basically "human-like" elves and "fairy-like" elves, meaning small ones. Both seem to exist within folklore depending on origin. I identified the creatures in the wardrobe as elves as a reference to "The Elves," which is a fairytale about a shoemaker who is very poor and helped by little elves who make shoes.

Selkie: The Selkie comes from Irish myths and legends. Their true form is that of a seal, but on land they can shed their skin and become human. If they do not have their seal skin, they cannot return to sea.

Faun: A half-human, half-goat creature. They are more like nature spirits, especially in reference to Greek mythology. In this retelling, I considered them a type of fae.

Fairyland: Reference to Irish fairy tales by W.B. Yeats in which he refers to the land of the fairies as Fairyland. In *Mountains Made of Glass*, all land inhabited by fae is considered Fairyland.

The Glass Mountains: The Glass Mountains take on various roles in fairytales across the world. They sprout trees with golden apples, offer refuge, or serve as an obstacle to the hero who must overcome them to obtain a princess (usually). Within Grimm fairytales, they appear in "The Iron Stove," "The Seven Ravens," "The Raven," "The Drummer," and "Old Rinkrank."

The Enchanted Forest: In fairytales, the Enchanted Forest is a symbol of change and transformation.

The Seven Brothers & Their Seven Kingdoms:

Casamir: The Kingdom of Thorn
Lore: The Kingdom of Nightshade
Silas: The Kingdom of Havelock
Eero: The Kingdom of Foxglove
Talon: The Kingdom of Hellebore
Cardic: The Kingdom of Larkspur
Sephtis: The Kingdom of Willowin

CHAPTER ONE
The Toad in the Well

The goose hung suspended by its feet from a low limb, bleeding into a bucket. Each wet plop of blood made me flinch, the sound inescapable even as I chopped wood to feed my hearth for the coming storm. The air had grown colder in the few minutes I had been outside, and yet perspiration beaded across my forehead and dampened all the parts of my body.

I was hot and the blood was dripping, and the strike of my ax sounded like lightning in the hollow where I lived before the Enchanted Forest. I could feel her gaze, a dark and evil thing, but it was familiar. I had been raised beneath her eyes. She had witnessed my birth, the death of my mother and father, and the murder of my sister.

Father used to say the forest was magic, but I believed otherwise. In fact, I did not think the forest was enchanted at all. She was alive, just as real and sentient as the fae who lived within. It was the fae who were magic, and they were as evil as she was.

My muscles grew more rigid, my jaw more tense, my mind spiraling with flashes of memories bathed in red as the blood continued to drip.

Plink.

A flash of white skin spattered with blood.

Plink.

Hair like spun gold turned red.

Plink.

An arrow lodged in a woman's breast.

But not just a woman—my sister.

Winter.

My chest ached, hollow from each loss.

My mother was the first to go on the heels of my birth. My sister was next, and my father followed shortly after, sick with grief. I had not been enough to save him, to keep him here on this earth, and while the forest had not taken them all by her hand, I blamed her for it.

I blamed her for my pain.

A deep groan shook the ground at my feet, and I paused, lowering my ax, searching the darkened wood for the source of the sound. The forest seemed to creep closer, the grove in which my house was nestled growing smaller and smaller day by day. Soon, her evil would consume us all.

I snatched the bucket from beneath the goose and slung the contents into the forest, a line of crimson now darkening the leaf-covered ground.

"Have you not had enough blood?" I seethed, my insides shaking with rage, but the forest remained quiet in the aftermath of my sacrifice, and I was left feeling drained.

"Gesela?"

I stiffened at the sound of Elsie's soft voice and waited until the pressure in my eyes subsided to face her, swallowing the hard lump in my throat. I would have called her a friend, but that was before my sister was taken by the forest, because once she was gone, everyone abandoned me. There was a part of me that could not blame Elsie. I knew she had been pressured to distance herself, first by her parents and then by the villagers who met monthly. They believed I was cursed to lose everyone I loved, and I was not so certain they were wrong.

Elsie was pale except for her cheeks which were rosy red. Her coloring made her eyes look darker, almost stormy. Her hair had come loose from her bun and made a wispy halo around her head.

"What is it, Elsie?"

Her eyes were wide, much like my sister's had been at death. Something had frightened her. Perhaps it had been me.

"The well's gone dry," she said, her voice hoarse. She licked her cracked lips.

"What am I supposed to do about it?" I asked, though her words carved out a deep sense of dread in the bottom of my stomach.

She paused for a moment and then said quietly, "It's your turn, Gesela."

I heard the words but ignored them, bending to pick up my ax. I knew what she meant without explanation. It was my turn to bear the consequences of the curse on our village, Elk.

Since I was a child, Elk had been under a curse of curses. No one agreed on how or why the curse began. Some blamed a merchant who broke his promise to a witch. Some said it was a tailor. Others said it was a maiden, and a few blamed the fae and a bargain gone wrong.

Whatever the cause, a villager of Elk was always chosen to end each curse—some as simple as a case of painful boils, others as devastating as a harvest destroyed by locust. It was said to be a random selection, but everyone knew better. The mayor of Elk used the curses to rid his town of those he did not deem worthy, because in the end, no villager could break a curse without a consequence.

Like my sister.

I brought my ax down, splitting the wood so hard, the blade cracked the log beneath.

"I do not use the well," I said. "I have my own."

"It cannot be helped, Gesela," Elsie said.

"But it is not fair," I said, looking at her.

Her eyes darted to the right. I froze and turned to see that the villagers of Elk had gathered behind me like a row of pale ghosts, save Sheriff Roland, who was at their head. He wore a fine uniform, blue like the spring sky, and his hair was golden like the sun, curling like wild vines.

The women of Elk called him handsome. They liked his dimpled smile and that he had teeth.

"Gesela," he said as he approached. "The well's gone dry."

"I do not use the well," I repeated.

His expression was passive as he responded, "It cannot be helped."

My throat was parched. I was well aware of how Elsie and Roland had positioned themselves around me,

4

Elsie to my back, Roland angled in front. There was no escape. Even if I had wanted, the only refuge was the forest behind me, and to race beneath its eaves was to embrace death with open arms.

I should want to die, I thought. It was not as if I had anything left, and yet I did not wish to give the forest the satisfaction of my bones.

I gathered my apron into my hands to dry my sweaty palms as Roland stepped aside, holding my gaze. Elsie's hand pressed into the small of my back. I hated the touch and I moved to escape it. Once I had passed Roland, he and Elsie fell into step behind me, herding me toward the villagers, who were as still as a fence row.

I knew them all, and their secrets, but I had never told them because they also knew mine.

No one spoke, but as I drew near, the people of Elk moved—some ahead, some beside, some behind, caging me.

Roland and Elsie remained close. My heart felt as though it were beating in my entire body. I thought of the other curses that had been broken. They were all so different. One villager had wandered through the Enchanted Forest and picked a flower from the garden of a witch. She cursed him to become a bear. In despair, he returned to Elk and was shot with an arrow through the eye. It was only after he died that we learned who he was. The next morning, a swarm of sparrows attacked the hunter who had killed the bear and pecked out his eyes.

There was also a tree that had once grown golden apples, but over time, it ceased to produce the coveted fruit. One day, a young man wandered through the village

5

and said a mouse gnawed at its roots. He claimed if we killed the mouse, the fruit would thrive, so our previous mayor killed the mouse, and the fruit returned. The mayor picked an apple, bit into it, and was consumed with such hunger, he gorged himself to death.

No one else touched the fruit of the tree or the mayor who died beneath its boughs.

There were no happy endings, that much I knew. Whatever I faced after this would surely lead to my death.

The villagers spilled into the center of town like phantoms. They kept me within their ghostly circle, surrounding the well, which was open to the sky and only a cold, stone circle that went deep into the ground. I approached and looked down, the bottom dry as a bone.

Roland stood beside me, too close, too warm.

"Who will you sacrifice when everyone you hate is dead?" I asked, looking at him.

"I do not hate you," Roland said, and his eyes dipped, glittering shamelessly as he stared at my breasts. "Quite the opposite."

Revulsion twisted my gut.

I had known Roland my whole life just as I knew everyone in Elk. He was the son of a wealthy merchant. That money had bought him status among the villagers and placed him at the mayor's side, which gave him power over every woman he ever laid eyes on and ensured he never had to face a curse.

My own misfortune had never deterred Roland. He had often offered to *help my case* if only I'd fuck him.

"You are disgusting."

"Oh, Gesela, do not pretend you despise my attention."

"I do," I said. "I am telling you."

Roland's face hardened, but he drew nearer, and it took everything in me not to push him away. I hated how he smelled, like wet hay and leather.

"I could make this go away. Say the word."

"What word?" I asked between my teeth.

"Say you will marry me."

I shoved him.

It was not as if he were serious either. He had made many proposals to women under the guise that he would save them, only to shame them later for believing he was serious.

If anyone was a curse on this land, it was Roland Richter.

"That is more than one word, idiot," I seethed. "But I shall give you one—never!"

Roland ground his teeth and then pushed me toward the well.

"Then you will face this curse."

I stumbled, catching myself against the side of the well, my palms braced against the slimy stone as I faced the endless darkness below.

"The crone in the wood says there is a toad in the well. Kill it and we will have water again."

"And did the crone say what will happen to me?"

"I gave you an out and you refused."

"You did not give me an out," I snapped. "You offered another curse."

"You think marriage to me is equal to what the forest would do?"

"Yes," I hissed. "I might consider it if I found you the least bit handsome, but as it is, I would vomit the moment your cock entered my body."

7

Roland snapped. I knew he was capable of violence. It was a truth that moved in his eyes.

He pushed me, and as my knees hit the back of the well, I tumbled over the edge and fell. The air was cold against my back, and I hit the bottom with a loud crack. I lay, quiet and stunned, blinking at the bright light streaming in from the round opening above. It seemed so far away, though my fall had been quick.

Elsie was the first to peer down, and when she caught sight of me, she covered her mouth and disappeared. Then there was Roland, who spit into the well.

"Elven bitch," he hissed.

I flinched at the words, which were just as painful as my fall.

Then they were gone.

I groaned and tried to sit up, but my back hurt and each breath I took was painful. A high-pitched trill made me jerk, sending a spasm of pain down my spine. I turned to find a large, bulbous toad staring at me, its round eyes glowing like lamplights in the dark.

I mourned that I had not killed the toad during my fall. At least then it would have been an accident.

"This is all your fault," I said.

The toad's answer was a shrieking call before it jumped.

I screamed, thinking it was about to leap on me, but saw that it landed on a piece of stone jutting from the side of the well.

I sat up slowly, groaning as the pain in my back constricted my lungs. The toad screamed again, throat bubbling. I considered killing it and looked at my feet, searching for a loose stone I might use to smash it, though the thought sent a wave of nausea through me. I might slaughter geese to eat, but a toad was different. This toad was different. It was the victim of this curse just as I was.

Another screech echoed loudly in the compact space, and I cringed.

When I looked back at the toad, it had moved farther up the wall, perched on another rock, waiting.

"Are you trying to escape me?" I asked.

Its answer was to turn, its webbed feet squelching against the rocky surface, and jump to another ledge. Once it was secured, it turned to look at me and offered another high-pitched shriek. I cringed at the sound as it surrounded me, my muscles tightening.

I suddenly wondered if this toad was trying to help me out of the well instead.

I approached and placed my foot on one of the rocks, gripping two others over my head. My heart raced as I searched for foot and hand holds, gripping frantically at slimy stones. The reach hurt my sides and stole my breath, but I managed to lift myself. As I did, the toad moved on, finding another ridge. I followed carefully, fingers freezing, legs shaking as threads of pain skittered down my spine.

The higher I climbed, the harder I clung to the stones for fear I would fall again. The weather had worsened since I'd been in the well, and sleet stung my face.

The toad reached the top before me, turning to stare with its large, yellow eyes before hopping out of sight. I was not far behind. Gripping the edge of the well with numb fingers, I managed to peer over and found the center of town deserted, likely because the storm had already arrived.

I was relieved, fearing that if Roland caught me climbing out of the well, he would only push me in again.

I let my stomach rest on the stone lip before sliding to the icy ground. There I lay, still and quiet, body racked with pain. Absently, I wondered what parts of me were broken. At the very least, I was badly bruised.

The toad waited patiently nearby, and as I stared up at the pale, gray sky, I wondered if anyone was watching me from the warmth of their home. Would they inform Roland? Had he assumed I was dead?

A now-familiar croak drew my attention, and I let my head fall in its direction, watching as the toad hopped onto the ledge of the well.

"No!"

I scrambled onto my knees and stumbled to my feet, bolting toward the toad, managing to grab its leg as it was about to jump back into the dark hole we had just left.

I threw it, and it soared over my head and landed on its back in the muddy square behind me. As if it felt no pain, it righted itself and started toward the well.

"I am trying to save you, you bastard," I said through my teeth, reaching for it again. Its body was slippery, which did not make it easy to hold as it wriggled in my grasp. "I'll keep you in a cage if I have to!"

I'd rather that than kill it.

The toad gave a keen cry just as my foot hit a patch of frozen ground. I fell onto my back again. I hardly had time to register the pain because the toad was free and already leaping frantically to the well.

A sharp twist of frustration spurred me on, and I

shifted onto my knees, crawling to reach it, but it was one hop ahead of me. I tried to get to my feet, but the ground was too slick, and I crashed to my knees.

I gritted my teeth, scowling as I moved over the ground, my palm slamming down on a sharp rock. I did not even care that it hurt. My fingers curled around it. It was heavier than I thought it would be, bigger too, and just as the toad returned to the well, I reached for it, yanked it to the ground, and brought the rock down on its head.

A heavy silence followed, pressing into my ears, filling my body with a strange sense of shock as I stared at the lifeless toad, its legs still twitching. I did not remove the rock because I did not want to face what I had done.

It wouldn't stop. Why wouldn't it stop?

But I knew the answer.

It was cursed. We were all cursed.

I vomited and the rancid smell continued to turn my stomach, even as I pulled off my apron and wrapped the toad and the rock in the fabric. I rose to my feet and stumbled home. The goose I had slaughtered earlier was long gone, likely pulled from its place by wolves.

I could not find it in me to care.

I grabbed my ax, still lodged in the log where I'd left it, and walked to the edge of the Enchanted Forest where I chopped into the hard ground, scraping mounds of dirt aside until I had formed a deep enough chasm to fit the toad inside. Once I covered its body in the hard dirt, I sat there on my knees, letting the sleet strike my body like small, sharp needles. It reminded me that I could feel.

After a while, I rose, and despite the cold, I made my

way to the rain barrel outside my house, breaking the sheet of ice that had formed over the top, and used the pan I kept inside to douse myself in water, washing my face and arms.

I brought the ax inside, leaving it on my bedside table before tending to the fire. I stripped off my sodden clothes and pulled on my nightgown before crawling into bed.

My head throbbed and my body ached as I curled into myself, shivering until I grew warm beneath my blankets.

I wondered if I would die in my sleep.

I hoped.

Because I knew something worse was coming for me.

CHAPTER TWO
Five Elven Princes

I woke up shivering.

Peeling open my bleary eyes, I saw the shutters were open and ice had gathered on the ledge. Despite the howling wind, my curtain hung stiff, frozen.

I frowned, confused. I had definitely latched the window.

The hair on the back of my neck rose, and gooseflesh trailed down my arms as a deep sense of fear ran my blood cold.

I was not alone.

I reach for my knife, which I kept beneath my pillow, but as my fingers brushed the hilt, it disappeared.

"Fuck!"

"Tsk, tsk, tsk," said a voice. "Such language."

I rolled onto my back, intending to reach for my ax, which rested on the bedside table where I left it, but my eyes caught on a figure leaning against the wall of my room. He was tall, thin, and ethereal. The tips of pointed ears peeked out from his long black hair, which slipped over his shoulder, as shiny as moonlight on dark water.

He wore a black wool overcoat trimmed in gold, leggings, and heavy black boots, the foot of one propped flat against the wall behind him.

He was an elf, and judging by the finery of his clothing, a lord.

"Fuck," I said again.

This wasn't good.

He, like all types of fae, had come from the Enchanted Forest. I had no doubt he had come to seek retribution for the toad I had killed.

A hand gripped my chin hard as something sharp trailed down the side of my face. Blood welled.

"Foul human," said another voice, a wet tongue skating over the wound. "Foul mouth."

I tried to move but couldn't and only managed to sink my nails into the arm of my attacker, dragging them downward.

I felt his skin gather beneath my nails, and the creature hissed, his hand tightening on my face as he jerked my head back.

Now I could see his face, which was similar to the other elven lord's, though somehow more vicious, and instead of dark hair, his was bright blond. His fingers dug into my jaw so hard, I thought he might tear it away.

"Release her, Sephtis," said a third voice.

But he did not loosen his hold. If anything, it tightened, and he bent over me, eyes boring into mine, irises red-tinged and unnerving.

"Why should I?" he asked, his voice so low it was as if he were posing the question to me.

A hand seemed to appear out of thin air and jerked Sephtis's free, and another elf came into view. This one looked the same as the first—dark-haired and beautiful. Only his eyes were different, a strange, mossy color, neither completely green nor completely brown.

"You were supposed to keep an eye on him, Lore," said the new elven lord, and I assumed he was talking to the first elf, the one who had taken my knife.

Sephtis glared.

"Here to spoil our fun, Silas?" he asked.

My stomach soured at Sephtis's idea of fun.

The blond jerked away and then fell into place between Lore and Silas. Two others had joined us since, one with amber-colored eyes and one who bore a deep scar on the left side of his face.

There were five of them in total. Five elven lords, four of whom were dark-haired, but they all looked the same, even the blond. The only variation was in their expressions, ranging from most severe to least. They stood at the end of my bed, blocking me in.

"Will anyone else be joining us?" I snapped, voice as frigid as my room.

"You could not handle any more of us, vicious thing," said Lore. "Careful what you wish for."

"I made no wish," I said vehemently. I knew the consequences of careless wishing and had seen it with my own eyes.

I wish you were dead! I had yelled at my sister, and then she was.

"She is a tiny thing," said Silas.

"A vicious thing," said Sephtis.

"She killed our brother," said the one with the scar.

"Your brother?" I asked, feeling the color drain from my face.

"Look, Talon! Her face is as pale as snow!" said Sephtis. He seemed the angriest and the scariest.

"You know of what we speak, human," said the one with amber eyes whose voice was quiet and calm.

"I did not kill an elf," I said.

"But you killed a toad," said Lore.

"Bashed him over the head with a rock," said Sephtis.

"You buried him at the edge of the Enchanted Forest," said Talon.

I swallowed a thickness that had gathered in my throat.

"I had no choice," I said, the words a fierce whisper. I knew they were futile. No one in Elk or the world beyond cared why I had done what I had done, only that there were consequences. "There was a curse."

"There is always a curse, always a choice," said Silas.

"You could have chosen to break our brother's curse rather than your town's curse," said Lore. "He would have made you his queen out of gratitude for your rescue."

"But alas, you bashed his brains instead, and so we must punish you," said Sephtis, a hungry glint in his red eyes.

"How was I to know he was anything but a toad?" I demanded.

"That is the folly of your human blood, to take everything as it appears and not as it is," said Silas.

"And is it the folly of elves to take everything as it is and not as it appears?"

"Foolish human," said Lore. "We have no flaws."

"Then how did your brother end up as a toad in a well?"

"He is no longer a toad in a well," said Talon. "He is dead in a hole."

All the elves spoke with a cold civility, save the one with amber eyes who had only spoken once since he arrived. They were not here because they loved their brother. This was about honor. It was the justice demanded by the Forest.

There was a beat of silence as the five elven lords exchanged looks.

"You shall spend six years as our seventh brother's prisoner," said Silas.

"I only count five of you," I said.

"Our seventh is a beast," said Sephtis, but I could not imagine anything more terrifying than him, who had cut me so easily and tasted my blood.

"He cannot be worse than all of you," I snapped, though dread seeped into my veins as I spoke those words. Somehow, I knew he was worse.

"I suppose you will find out," said Silas.

There was a beat of silence as I stared at the five, uncertain of what happened now. Would they march me through the forest to the doorstep of their seventh brother's kingdom?

"Where is your seventh brother?" I asked, considering how quickly I could reach for my ax, which still sat on the table near my bed. I could feel its presence burning my skin, I wanted it in hand so badly. "Why is he not here?"

"No one has seen the Thorn Prince, not in nearly ten years," said Lore.

"How can you be certain he is a beast?"

"Because we're all beasts," said Sephtis, a smirk on his face.

I reached for my ax.

The movement sent a shock of pain up my side. It squeezed my lungs and held on to my breath, making me dizzy. Still, I shot to my feet, unsteady on the lumpy bed, and lifted the ax over my head, angling for the elf closest to me, when a great wave of magic hit me square in the chest.

I fell, but instead of my knees striking the hard floor of my room, I hit lush carpet. Despite the softer landing, every injured part of my body screamed and a pained cry tore from deep in my throat.

It was too late to swallow, and still I slammed my mouth shut, grinding my teeth against the pain, though it was nothing compared to the sudden sense of dread that numbed my body as a cold, sensual voice dripped over my skin.

"Well, what have we here?"

Slowly, my gaze rose over shiny black boots and well-muscled legs clad in black leggings. They were so tight, they left nothing to the imagination. My eyes widened at the indecent outline of his cock, something that would normally be covered by a long tunic, except he was shirtless, the hard lines of his abs and powerful shoulders on display, obscured only by a ring and a white tooth which hung at the end of two silver chains.

I took him in—all of him—before meeting his gaze.

Black eyes stared back, and while it felt ridiculous to say, they were so dark, they felt almost endless like the well. A sudden fear seized me, an instinctive knowledge that if I drew too close, I might fall into those eyes.

This was the seventh brother—the beast.

He looked like his siblings, the dark-haired ones, but there was still something different about him, something harder and darker. His forehead was high, his cheekbones too, and his lips were full and colorless.

He was beautiful and cold, like winter in Elk.

My fingers closed around the handle of my ax, and I rose to my feet.

"Stay back!"

His lips curled into a wicked grin.

"Oh, vicious creature," he said. "Are you here to kill me?"

"If you give me a reason," I replied, tightening my hold.

"I could give you three."

"I do not need three," I said. "One will suffice."

He chuckled quietly, never losing that mischievous glint in his eyes.

"One then," he said, and his smile slowly faded. "Kill me...before I kill you."

His words hit harder than my fall down the well, and before I lifted my ax, he was behind me, his hand on my throat. I could feel his long nails pressing into my skin. He drew my head back to the point that I thought my neck would break.

Several sharp pricks stung my palm, and I hissed at the pain, dropping my ax. The handle had grown thorns. With my hands free, I reached for the beast's at my throat, but even as I sunk my own nails into his skin, he did not move.

"Vicious thing," he said, and I could feel his lips against my cheek. "Vicious fae."

"*Don't* call me that," I said between my teeth.

He chuckled, fingers pressing deeper.

"Which word? Vicious or fae?"

Being fae, no matter how little, had never served me. The villagers whispered that my blood had killed my mother and it had not saved my sister from the forest.

It had, though, ensured I would always be alone. I had no family, no friends, no lovers.

The prince's voice rumbled against my skin, and I felt it in my chest. He spoke slowly, his lips trailing along my jaw, and I hated the way it made me feel, too conscious of the emptiness between my thighs, of the heat roiling in my gut, fueled by the press of his cock against my ass.

I hated it, and yet I pressed into him harder. I almost wished he would hurt me so I could stop these awful feelings firing through my veins.

"You *know* which word," I seethed, my voice fierce but quiet. I could not speak any louder. I could barely breathe.

"But you are fae," he said.

"Not enough to tell," I said.

I was not even sure when my blood had come to mix with the fae I only knew it had been many great-grandfathers ago. No matter how many years passed, the people of Elk remembered, and the fae, they always *knew*.

"Enough for me to taste."

His free hand splayed across my hip, and my nails bit into him to keep from guiding him lower, to the heat between my legs.

"Tell me, she who does not wish to be fae, why have you come?"

"I didn't…not of my own accord," I said.

"Do you want to know what I think?"

I swallowed hard, and the pressure of his hand was heavy against my throat.

"I'd rather you let me go."

"You shouldn't lie to an elven prince," he said, and his hand began to gather the hem of my shift. My muscles tightened even more, screaming as I remained against him.

"What makes you think I'm lying?"

"Shall I give you three reasons?" he asked.

"One will suffice," I said again, though I could barely recall what he had said or what I had wanted to say, my mind so clouded with a lustful wish to feel him inside me.

Wish.

Great consequences came from careless wishes, even unspoken. One never knew who was listening, even to thoughts.

"Not once have you tried to run," he said.

For the first time, I jerked in his arms.

"Ah, ah, ah, vicious creature," he said, and suddenly he was in front of me, his hand never leaving my neck as he guided me back, pinning me against a wall. Every part of his body rested against mine, hard and aroused, and I was a willing prisoner to it, melting into something soft and supple.

I did not recognize myself.

"Answer my question. Bend to my will. Why have you come, sweet one?"

As he spoke, his lips touched my cheek.

"I told you—"

He pulled away, and I met his endless dark eyes.

"Not of your own accord but someone's. Whose?"

"If you cannot guess, then perhaps you have no right to know."

"No right?" he asked and inclined his head. "Bold words, vicious one, when you are in my kingdom, beneath my roof, within my arms."

I glared at him and jerked on his arm, his hand still around my neck.

"I would hardly call *this* in your arms."

He smirked and leaned in, his breath hot against my ear. "And yet you respond."

Then his lips touched my skin, and I held my breath, pressing my head into the wall as hard as I could.

"Hmm, you are sweet," he said, his tongue tasting. "I could eat you whole."

His free hand had gone to the hem of my nightgown again. His fingers slipped between my thighs, but he did not move to the place where I ached. I felt ashamed because he had to feel the heat radiating from me. I felt it everywhere.

"Are you wet for me, vicious creature?"

I kept my eyes shut, my fingers digging into his skin. I wanted to beg for his touch just as much as I wanted to bury an ax in his chest.

The beast lifted my leg and hitched it over his hip, leaning into me. His hard cock pressed into me, coaxing a harsh sound from deep in my throat. Our mouths opened against each other. For a brief second, his tongue darted out to taste mine, and then he chuckled.

His laugh slithered over me, feeding both my anger and embarrassment.

I took that moment to charge, pushing him away so violently, he stumbled back enough for me to bolt. I snatched my ax from the floor and fled the room, but as soon as I was out the door, I found myself in a hallway that looked like a wooded lane. My feet now raced over cold ground, past several naked trees that seemed to bow over me. Where before I had been warm within the elf lord's room, here, the wind whipped me, each cold lash making me tremble.

There was a part of me that did not understand how I had seemed to be within the walls of a castle and was now suddenly running through the woods, but I also knew I had no time to question the magic of the Thorn Prince's kingdom.

I had to run as far away as possible before he caught me.

As I ran, the path grew narrow, as if the trees were creeping closer. Soon there was no path at all, only the leaf-ridden floor of a wooded forest. Above me, the trees groaned and reached for me, their great limbs coming down on me like clawed fingers. They scratched and split my skin, and I swiped at them with my ax, but some still managed to become tangled within my shift and tore the thin fabric. My sleeve hung off my shoulder, the neckline gaped, and the hem was in tatters. Still, I managed to free myself, escaping the vile wood as it let out into a field that looked more like an endless ocean, the night too dark to see what lay at my feet, but I could feel it.

The ground was tender and wet, and my feet sank in cold mud. I could barely stay upright. I slipped and my ankle twisted. The pain sent me to the ground, and

I landed hard on my hands and knees when something sharp wrapped around my legs and squeezed. I screamed and rolled onto my back as thorned vines crawled up my legs, digging deep into my skin. They slithered up my body until they were wrapped around my wrists, holding them over my head, and suddenly, I was face-to-face with the beast.

The prince hovered over me, his face inches from mine, the pendants of his necklaces rested against my chest. Instead of thorns, his fingers dug into my wrists, and his ankles were tangled with mine.

"My brothers sent you," he said and rested his body against mine. "Are you a spy?"

"Do I look like a spy?" I spat.

His eyes dropped to my breasts, exposed. My nipples had pebbled, hard from the cold, hard from his gaze, which flashed as it returned to mine.

"You look like a distraction."

"Then perhaps you should let me go," I said.

"I cannot let you go," he said. "You must earn your right to be free."

"My *right*?" I asked, the words fierce. I lifted my head, drawing closer to him, lips nearly touching. "I was sent here against my will."

"You were sent here as my prisoner," he said. "Which will it be, vicious one? Six years with me or a chance to be free?"

I glared at him, breathing hard.

"If you knew, why didn't you lock me up from the start?"

He smirked. "Who said I keep my prisoners locked up?"

"Where do you keep them then?"

"Shouldn't you ask where I will keep you?"

I did not answer, and the longer he stared at me, the more I wished to disappear. Perhaps the ground would open up and swallow me whole so I would not have to face how I felt beneath him.

After a few seconds, he spoke.

"Guess my true name," he said.

I blinked. "What?"

"You have seven days to guess my true name, and I will set you free."

I took several deep breaths as I processed his proposal. I was not so eager to be free that I would blindly jump at the first offer. All deals with fae—especially elves—were traps.

"How many guesses do I have?"

"As many as you wish," he said.

"I do not speak in wishes," I said.

He raised a brow. "Don't you?"

I ground my teeth. "Say it another way."

He chuckled. "As many as you would like."

"Will you keep count?"

He smirked.

"Clever creature," he said. "Of course."

"I thought so."

I would have to be careful with my answers and keep them to a minimum.

"And if I fail?"

"Then you fail," he said. "And you will be my prisoner for six years, plus one year more for every wrong answer you give."

"And what are the consequences of guessing correctly?"

His smile turned wicked, his gaze shrewd, and I caught a glimpse of what lurked beneath his skin—perhaps the true beast.

"Speak my name and find out."

I stared at him, weighing my options, all with dire consequences.

Even if I did manage to guess the beast's name correctly, what sort of evil would I unleash?

And did it really matter if I was free?

"I'll guess your name," I said.

His answer was a grin.

CHAPTER THREE
The Beast

The beast released my wrists, and I shoved my hands against his chest, but he vanished.

I sat up.

Where had he gone?

I tried to stand, but my ankle was swollen and bruised. I rolled onto my hands and knees and struggled to my feet, finding that I was now in what appeared to be the entrance of a castle, my eyes narrowing on a door.

I stumbled toward it and fell, moving too quickly for my injured ankle.

"Perhaps you should stay there," said the beast, and I looked up from the floor into his dark eyes. He stood guard at the door, looking far larger than he had before. "Your knees seem to like it."

"Fuck you."

"You will," he said. "Far sooner than you think if you leave my castle."

I felt the color drain from my face, and it seemed to

spark joy in the beast's eyes. Until his gaze lowered. I was covered in mud, and now that I was inside and warm, it was drying on my skin.

"Bathe," he said. "You look and smell like a pig."

I glared, rising to my feet and crossing my arms over my chest. It seemed ridiculous to hide now, but his sudden cold demeanor reminded me how silly I had been this evening. I should have tried to kill him the moment I met his gaze. Instead, I'd let him touch me and it had done nothing but give him power over me.

My mouth twisted into a disgusted smile.

"Do I repulse you?" I asked, gleeful at the thought.

He arched a brow.

"Clearly not."

I kept his gaze, unwilling to let my eyes wander, knowing well enough what he meant. I could still feel the hard press of his cock against me.

Perhaps he wasn't the only one with power here.

I looked around the entryway, which was dark despite several lit candles waning away in corners, noticing that flowering vines covered the walls and draped from the ceiling. Behind me was a staircase covered in moss, the rails tangled in trailing vines, creating a path to a second floor that looked like the dark woods of the Enchanted Forest.

I was no longer surprised that I had found myself outside once I had left the beast's room. It seemed that his entire castle was a forest.

"Where do you suggest I bathe?" I asked.

"Before me," he said, and once again, my surroundings changed. Suddenly, I was in a large, cavernous room. Water wept from the rocky walls of a grotto into a dark pool overflowing into a small stream that disappeared into the darkness of the room.

I turned to face the beast, furious.

"I will not bathe in front of you," I said.

"If you will not bathe in front of me, then you will bathe in front of them," he said, inclining his head to the darkness of the room, which was lit by several pairs of red eyes. Awful, raspy laughs followed, and the creatures in the shadow came into the light.

The eyes belonged to several short goblins with long, sharp teeth and taloned fingers. Their hair was long and scraggly, more akin to the roots of an old tree. On their heads were pointed caps, red from blood, which they had let mat their hair and drip down their faces.

I swallowed a scream and scowled at him.

"I would rather die," I said.

"Suit yourself," said the beast with a lazy shrug of his shoulder, and then he vanished, leaving me to face the bloodied creatures. They scowled, red eyes alight and angry as they melded with the dark once more. For a brief moment, I thought they might leave me alone—until one launched a stone at my head.

I managed to dodge it, only to be hit square in the face by another.

Blood gushed from my nose, and I hid my face as more rocks pummeled my body.

"Fine! Fine, you miserable fuck!" I screamed. "I'll bathe in front of you!"

The attack stopped, and when I uncovered my head, I found the elven lord had returned. He stood near, a smug expression on his pretty face.

"I suppose I should have mentioned that the red caps throw stones," he said.

I glared as I rose to my feet and spit blood in his face. "I hate you."

He did not wipe his face or approach me. Instead, he smiled, wicked and cruel.

"Oh, vicious thing, you do not know hate. Give me time."

I had never felt so murderous and wondered what the consequences were of killing two elven lords. My thoughts were interrupted when another rock flew from the dark. This time, the beast snatched it within his clawlike hand, lobbing it back. A loud crack followed, and one of the red caps fell facedown, blood pooling around its head. Seconds after, taloned hands tugged him back into the shadow while they muttered angry curses.

No more rocks were thrown.

The beast looked at me.

"Bathe. They will not bother you so long as I am here."

"Will they watch?"

"Likely," he said. "But do not worry. They will lust only for your blood, not your body."

I pressed my lips thin and then looked at the pool. It was slightly elevated, accessed only by a set of narrow steps. I considered refusing the bath altogether, but one glance down my front only made me want it more. The mud made it hard to tell just how injured I truly was—not just my ankle but my entire body. Not to mention the blood from my nose was drying on my face and chest.

I approached the pool, eyeing the water. Would a sprite surge from its depths and drown me? Did I really care? It had never occurred to me until now that I had little to fight for beyond myself. What freedom lay beyond these walls but loneliness?

I shrugged off what remained of my nightgown and took the steps slowly, and though I led with my uninjured ankle, keeping weight on the other was near unbearable. I started to kneel, thinking that I might be able to crawl over the edge of the pool, when the beast offered his hand, long nails like sharp blades. Tired and not wishing to injure myself further, I took it. He held my fingers and I slipped into the pool.

The water was not as deep as I had hoped, hitting midthigh. I waded until I was at the center and then turned and held the beast's gaze as I settled into the pool. The water was surprisingly warm, and while it soothed, it also drew attention to how much I ached.

I took a breath, moaning as I exhaled.

"Did my brothers hurt you?" he asked.

He had not taken his eyes off me, and there was a harshness to his face. If I had to guess, he was asking because of the bruises blooming across my body.

"No. Your brothers were not the first unfortunate thing to befall me today...or perhaps that was yesterday."

I did not know the time and I did not explain further—not the curse of the well or even the toad, because none of it mattered. None of it was going to change my present or my future.

The beast did not ask.

"Is this what it means to be your prisoner?" I asked. "To never have a moment of privacy?"

"Do you wish to be stoned to death?"

"Do red caps lurk in every corner of your castle?"

He smirked but did not answer.

"I will give you a moment's peace once you are safely in your room."

"My room?"

"Your cell, your prison," he said. "Call it what you wish, but I assume you understand the importance of staying inside until daybreak?"

I glared.

Night itself was dangerous, but night in the Enchanted

Forest was a death wish. When I was younger, foolish boys would dare each other to spend the night in the woods, never to be heard from again no matter how close they stayed to the border.

Sometimes the bodies were found in the daylight, beaten and broken or stripped to the bone. Others were not found at all, and I often wondered if they had been whisked away to another kingdom only to become slaves or concubines to some great fae ruler.

"And after daybreak?"

"You may go wherever you dare, but only when I have no use for you."

I ground my teeth. "What use?"

"Whatever I desire," he said. "You are my prisoner."

"And if I refuse?"

"You will always have a choice," he said.

I knew what he meant by choice. It was either allow him to watch me bathe or be stoned to death.

I studied him for a moment and then fell back into the water. I scrubbed my face and my hair, and when I was finished, I remained below the surface, letting the air escape my mouth until my lungs burned and the water felt heavy, like the walls of an iron coffin.

Hands clamped down on my arms, and I opened my eyes, taking a deep, gasping breath as I broke the surface. The beast glared down at me, eyes shining with acute anger.

"You do not get to leave this world of your own accord," he said, his gaze falling to my lips. "And if you manage it, I will follow you in death and haunt you for all of eternity."

I was confused by his fierce response but had no time

to process his anger when he released me. I reached for him as I fell, but there was nothing to hold on to. He had already vanished. I landed on something soft—a bed, I realized as I sat up, still wet and naked.

I scanned the room. It was small, far narrower than it was wide. There was an uncovered window to the left and a hearth to the right, a fire crackling and popping within, making the room almost too warm. I slipped off the bed, and there was soft carpet at my feet. I paused for a moment and then bent to touch it with my hands. I had never felt anything like it. I had only ever known the feel of compacted dirt and the occasional handwoven rug.

If this was to be my cell, it was luxurious.

A tapping sound drew my attention. For one heart-stopping moment, I thought someone was at the window, but when I looked, it was only the trees rattling in the wind, and I could see nothing beyond the thick foliage and the deep night. There was a part of me that was unnerved by the obstruction. I'd have liked to look upon the beast's kingdom. At the same time, I was grateful and hopeful that it meant no one could peer in on me.

With that thought, I crossed to the door and tried the knob, ensuring it was locked, and then dragged a large wooden chest in front of it. I was aware of what the elven lord had not said—while I should not leave this room, he'd never said anything about someone coming in.

With the door barricaded, I returned to the bed and slipped beneath the covers and fell into a deep sleep.

CHAPTER FOUR

Mirror, Mirror

The creature in my castle is a seductress. She smells like sweet roses, and she clings to me like the cold despite the fire she's started in my blood. I want her. The need for her runs deep in my veins. It goes beyond soothing the swell of my cock.

In her presence, I can taste *freedom.*

"You will be the death of her."

"Did I summon you?" I asked, turning toward the jagged piece of mirror on my wall. It was one of seven pieces, the other six belonging to my brothers.

I could not see my reflection as I glared at him. He had made his visage dark, which was usual. When the mirror was clear, it meant anyone with another piece could spy. Though it was not as if I minded. My brothers would likely only catch me participating in various lascivious acts.

"You do not have to summon me. I am always watching."

"Charming," I said. "Will you linger while I pleasure myself too?"

"I have little choice. I am only a mirror."

"Suit yourself," I said, reaching for my erection, which strained against the fabric of my trousers. I had no shame, but before I had a chance to touch myself, the mirror spoke.

"Do you really think this mortal will learn your true name?"

I curled my fingers into a fist. "I would not have chosen her for the task if she did not show promise."

"You did not *choose*," the mirror drawled. "Your brothers *sent* her."

"It does not matter how she came to me. She is here. She is flesh and blood. She can set me free."

"*If* she falls in love with you."

"A small detail," I said.

"Small?" the mirror repeated with some surprise. "I would hardly call that detail small."

"I do not wish to speak on it," I said, my voice harsh, and my mood darkened, descending like shadow in the dying dusk.

I knew the mirror was right.

I needed her to love me, but I had waited nearly ten years for someone to come along with enough reason to learn my true name. This creature, she wished to be free, and if she wished hard enough, she might just set me free too.

"Do you truly believe they would send you a clever thing?"

"Perhaps you could tell me," I said. "Do you not exist in six other palaces and know all my brothers' secrets?"

"Five," he said, a reminder that one of my brothers was dead and that someone already had his piece of the enchanted mirror. It had once been whole and hung in our father's hall, but as he neared death, he broke it into seven pieces, one for each of his sons, and declared that whoever put it back together again would be king of the Enchanted Forest. "I only exist with five of your brothers now."

"Which of them managed to snatch Eero's piece?"

"None," said the mirror.

"None?" I asked, arching a brow. "Who has it now?"

"A pretty, petty thing."

"Hmm."

That will make things interesting for the others, I thought.

Especially Silas, who, of all my brothers, desired to be king most. Personally, I did not care for the crown, but I did not wish to give up my mirror either. He was a gateway, a portal to other parts of the Enchanted Forest.

That was the kind of power I wished to keep.

"You do not seem at all concerned," the mirror observed.

"I find it difficult to be concerned with anything beyond myself at this moment."

The mirror did not have expressions, but I could feel his disgust.

"You would think you would worry more about your life than your cock."

"I was talking about my life," I snapped. "But thank you for reminding me of my intention to fuck myself."

"To the image of your brother's murderer?" the mirror asked.

"Yes," I hissed.

I would have thanked her for it had I not wished to tangle her in my web.

Eero might be my brother, but blood meant nothing unless it was spilled in the Enchanted Forest, and at that point, it was currency.

Good fucking riddance, I thought, though it was not as if he would not be born again as all fae were. He'd likely crawl from the bell of a foxglove, as poisonous as ever.

Thinking of my brother darkened my mood.

"Show me the woman," I commanded, wishing to rekindle the desire that had inflamed my veins.

The mirror brightened, and now I looked on the vicious creature who had disturbed my night. She lay on her back, her arms splayed. She looked pale, even with the warmth of the fire igniting her limbs, though it did make her blond hair look ablaze.

I clenched my jaw, frustrated at how easily she slumbered, not at all caught in the throes of arousal like me.

Cruel creature.

It made me doubt she could love me at all, doubt that she could end this curse bestowed on me by the Glass Mountains.

"I need her to love me," I said.

"Love is learned," said the mirror. "Has it ever occurred to you that is the lesson the Glass Mountains hoped to teach you when they cursed you?"

I knew what the mountains were doing, but it was no lesson.

It was vengeance.

The Glass Mountains were a source of life within the Enchanted Forest, and they called the beings that sprang from their depths their *offspring*. What was born of them was immortal and moral.

I was immortal and immoral, born from the earth, and after I mixed my blood with one of their own, the Mountains cursed me to forget my true name unless it was spoken by my *one true love*.

That was nine years and three weeks ago.

I had one more week until I forgot my true name forever—until everyone forgot.

And if my name was forgotten, *I* was forgotten.

A name precedes you, and without one, you are nothing.

It was the truth of our world.

"A fool's errand," I said even as I stood before the mirror, aching and yearning for this creature in a way I had never before.

"For a foolish prince," said the mirror.

I might have reacted to his comment had the creature not rolled to her side. I was given a view of the dark bruises blooming across her back, reminding me that she had come to me injured.

My brothers were despicable creatures, but they would not have harmed her...physically at least.

My head became hot with rage.

"Show me who hurt her," I said, and the mirror rippled. My creature vanished and a man came into view. He was in bed, hovering over a woman, thrusting into her. She writhed beneath him, moaning in false pleasure.

I wondered why he had hurt my creature and if he had thought long it.

I drew nearer, pressing a clawed finger to the vision, anger gnashing my teeth.

"Fragile man," I growled. "I will break you."

The image went dark, and my reflection peered back at me, fierce and feral. The mirror laughed.

"Your lust is making you reckless."

"It is not reckless to make a mortal swallow his cock for hurting a woman," I said, and a slow grin spread across my face as I imagined the horror and pain that would contort the man's face. "It is...satisfying."

"You cannot curse anyone while you are cursed," said the mirror.

As if I had forgotten.

"I can be patient," I said.

I would take great pleasure in wounding the man who had wounded her—if she helped me end this cruel curse.

"You will be the death of her," the mirror said again.

"You are not a mirror of prophecy."

"I am a mirror of truth," he said.

I turned and crossed to my bed, and as I rested on the coverlet and took my aching length in hand, I thought of the creature and her rose-smelling hair and recalled how she fit against me. I pumped my hand faster, a little harder, until my head teemed with fantasies about how I would fuck her when she finally gave in.

"She will live. Long enough to speak my name," I said between clenched teeth just before I came.

I waited for sleep to take hold, but instead of my limbs growing heavy and my eyes sliding shut, my muscles grew tight, and my body filled with blood as if I had not found release at all.

"No." I sat up.

Vicious creature.

Vicious brothers.

They had sent me a siren.

CHAPTER FIVE
The Selkie

When I woke up the next morning, my head ached and my mouth was dry. Blindly, I reached for the water I usually kept at my bedside, but instead of finding the handle of my mug, I touched something cold and slimy.

A scream tore from my throat, and I sat up to a chorus of snickers. My hand was covered in mucus, the table beside my bed crawling with slugs.

I was not home but in the palace of an elven prince, and there was a troupe of tiny pixies in my room. They hovered, wings vibrating. Some were naked while others wore tattered and dirty clothing.

I threw a pillow at them as I scrambled out of my bed, relieved my ankle bore little pain as I put pressure on my foot.

"If I get my hands on any of you, I will pluck your wings from your bodies and wear them as a crown!"

They laughed merrily, zipping close to my face as they scattered, flying out a crack in the window I had not noticed the night before. I glared after them and the door clicked open. My gaze shifted to the beast who filled the doorway.

For a moment, I was shocked that he was able to enter. I had pushed a chest in front of the doors last night, except now I found that it had been moved.

I gritted my teeth.

Those pixies would pay if I caught them in my room again.

The elven king looked cold and pale, his eyes severe and his mouth tight.

I could feel his disgust, and yet his gaze raked over my bare body.

"Picking fights?" he asked as his eyes met mine.

I started to respond when a short, stout brownie pushed her way into the room, grumbling as she went. Her ears were pointed and large, hanging off the sides of her face as if they were too heavy for her head. She wore a brown dress and a stained white apron.

I reached for the blanket on the bed and held it to myself.

The beast smirked.

"This is Naeve," he said. "She will help you prepare for the day."

"Prepare for the day?"

"You are welcome to remain as you are," he said, his eyes appraising. "Though I must admit, I quite like being the only one to see you like this."

"How do you know you are the only one?"

The beast narrowed his eyes.

"He isn't," said the brownie, who stood at my feet and ripped the blanket away. I rolled my fingers into

43

fists and growled at her as she made her way around me, her eyes assessing, but in a different way than the elven prince, who had taken a seat across the room, reclining comfortably, obviously intent on watching me *prepare for the day*, whatever that meant.

Once Naeve had made several rounds at my feet, she walked to the wooden wardrobe and knocked twice. One of the doors flew open, and a small creature poked its head out.

Naeve spoke to it in a language I did not understand. It was fast and so harsh, I thought they might be fighting. The small creature turned its attention to me for a moment. It had large round eyes that were set close and deep and a long, crooked nose that stuck out over a wide mouth.

It blinked at me, eyes shining incandescently, and then disappeared into the wardrobe, slamming the door. I took that to mean whatever Naeve had asked was unceremoniously rejected, but the brownie was not deterred. She crossed to a mirrored vanity, climbing onto the cushioned seat and the tabletop. Then she turned and pointed at the bench.

"Sit!"

I hesitated, gaze shifting between the beast and the brownie. When I did not move, Naeve kicked a small bowl of powder off the vanity.

"Sit!"

The prince laughed.

"Forgive her," he said, and at first, I thought he was talking to me, but I noticed that he was looking at Naeve as he continued. "She is a bit dull."

Naeve snickered and I scowled.

"I can take care of myself."

"Are you saying you asked me to watch you bathe because you wanted me to and not because you feared the red caps?"

"I hate you," I seethed, holding his gaze as I sat for Naeve, wondering what more I had to fear from the brownie or the creatures in my wardrobe.

His grin was menacing, and I ground my teeth, keeping them clenched as the brownie began to pull and twist strands of my hair. The beast watched, and for a brief moment, a harsh intensity returned to his face. I had no chance to study it or to think long on what had sparked it when he turned away, wandering toward the window from which the pixies had escaped.

"Must you remain?" I asked.

"Must you speak?" he returned.

"I suppose not, but then I would never utter your true name."

His jaw ticked. That was the only indication I had that my words affected him. He continued to stare out the window while I sat naked and Naeve plaited my hair. As soon as she finished, the doors to the wardrobe burst open, and a ball of fabric came flying toward me, landing on my head.

"Dress!" Naeve ordered.

I pulled the cloth off my head, a perpetual scowl on my face. I held up the fabric to find that the creatures in the closet had made a dress. The top was white and billowy, the skirt pale green, overlain with sheer white fabric. When I glance over at the prince, his back was still turned to me, so I stepped into the dress and reached behind to button up the back but found I could only clasp a few on my own.

I turned to look for Naeve, but she was gone.

Then I felt warm fingers take over, and I stiffened as the prince fastened my dress. Once he was finished, I turned to face him. He stared down at me and spoke, giving me no time to react to his intrusion.

"You are permitted to wander within my castle and my grounds, but go beyond the wall, and you may become another person's prisoner."

"Is there anyone worse than you?" I asked.

The beast lifted his hand and caressed the side of my face.

"Vicious creature, there is always something worse."

I held my breath beneath his touch, and when his hand fell away, the tension returned to my body.

"You will call me Casamir," he said. "It is my mortal name."

"I prefer beast," I said, suddenly aware of how much I had to crane my neck just to meet his gaze at this proximity.

His lips quirked and his hand snaked behind my neck and into my hair, fingers grazing my scalp. He had moved fast, and once he was close, my body warmed against his.

"Call me beast again," he said, his lips hovering over mine, "and I'll show you why I was given that name."

I could not help it. His threat provoked me, and a slow smile spread across my face.

"Beast," I whispered, and the prince's hand caught my throat. The black of his irises leaked into the whites of his eyes. He pushed me until I met the edge of the vanity, his hips pressed between my thighs.

I reached for his arm, but as I did, black tendrils rose from his skin and wrapped around my hands, becoming solid like the spindly branches of a bodark tree. They crawled over me, around my shoulders and down my back, wrapping around my waist. At the same time, another set of vines trailed up my legs, curling around my thighs, inching closer to the part of me that had ached for him last night. Even now, my body grew heavy and warm, wet for this cruel creature.

"Do not test me, vicious creature. I will swallow you whole."

I believed he could.

I wished he would.

We stared at each other for a long moment, and I felt like a spider caught in a web as the elven prince drew nearer. His free hand moved down the side of my body before gathering my skirt. I shivered as the fabric rose, exposing my leg, and when his hand landed high on my bare hip, my breath caught in my throat.

He never looked away from me, his eyes still drowning in black, his mouth hovering close to mine. I would be lying if I did not admit how desperately I wanted to know the feel of his lips against mine.

"Say my name," he said, the words a slow command. "My mortal name."

Silence spread between us, and his fingers were close to my heat, with the palm of his hand pressed flat against my ass. My heart beat fast in my chest like fluttering fairy wings, and my muscles grew taut. If I said his name, would he touch me instead of teasing me?

"What will you give me?" I asked.

He reared back only a fraction, as if realizing he had

shown too much surprise. He studied me, eyes narrowed, before the corner of his lip curled.

"What do you desire?"

As if he thought he could guess, his fingers pressed harder into my skin.

"A number," I said.

His brows lowered, confused. "A number?"

"How many letters are in your true name?"

He stared and I could tell he was displeased with me. Had he hoped I might ask for his touch? I doubted he mourned that I hadn't, more that I had not fallen for his seduction.

"Tricky creature," he said, and this time, his fingers pressed against my throat, his lips grazing across my lower jaw to my ear where he whispered, "Seven."

As he pulled back, his fiery eyes met mine. He loosened his hold on my neck, and the blood that had built in my head rushed away. I was dizzy and far more desperate than before to feel him inside me.

"Are you lying?" I asked, breathless.

Seven brothers. Seven years. Seven letters.

"I cannot lie," he said, and I knew that was true.

I started at him and then his mouth.

"I am waiting, vicious creature."

I stared at him a moment longer, searching his endless eyes, tracing his high cheekbones and arrogant smile. I leaned up and I could feel his breath on my lips. I wanted to taste his mouth, suck his tongue like a sweet sugarplum. I wanted him to writhe against me.

"Casamir."

I hadn't had any idea how his name would sound when it escaped my mouth, but it was so wrapped up in my desperate emotions, it sounded like a plea. There was a part of me that hoped it would work like a spell and break his control.

But he did not shiver or swallow. He did not press into me or tighten his hold.

He did lean in, and he moved his hand from my neck before pressing his lips to my throat, speaking in a hushed tone.

"Come when I call, sweet one."

Then he vanished.

I remained against the vanity, mind scrambling to make sense of what had just transpired between me and the elven prince. My heart was still racing, and I could feel his phantom hands and the vines against my skin.

I should not have been surprised by his power. He had used it on my ax when thorns had sprouted from the handle and later when he tripped me as I fled into the enchanted night. But was that the power that made him a beast? Or was it something else entirely?

My gaze shifted as I caught movement from the window. The pixies I had chased from my room were gathered there, faces pressed against the glass.

I scowled and marched toward them, snatching the pillow from the floor I had thrown earlier and launching it at them. I knew it would do no good—they were on the other side of the glass—but it felt good to throw something.

The pillow landed with a soft plop and fell to the floor. The pixies giggled and flew off. I wondered what they had seen and who they might tell. Though it was more likely they just perceived me as another stupid mortal who had fallen for a pretty elven prince.

My gaze fell and I noticed that the broken window that had allowed the pixies entrance to my room was now mended, and while I'd have liked to feel a sense of gratitude toward the prince for the fix, dread filled my stomach like a bitter poison.

Elves did no favors.

What more did I owe the Prince of Thorns?

I left my room with some hesitation, uncertain of what I would find on the other side. I wanted to bring my ax, but the handle was still covered in thorns and impossible to hold. Even without a weapon, I did not wish to remain indoors. It was not in my nature, even when I resided in my cottage on the edge of the forest, even hating that whatever lurked between her branches watched. Worse, what would watch me within the beast's—*Casamir's*—realm?

My door opened to a stone hallway, the walls of which were covered in vines that flowered as I walked by.

Charming, I thought, except that the vines had thorns and they were red-tipped, as if each had pricked a person and drawn blood, and the flowers, which were white and pink and bell-shaped, were poisonous to the touch—a virtual death trap.

I followed them, careful not to knock into the wall. The hallway curved to the right, and I found myself on a portico lined with stone columns, wrapped in the same flowering vines. Beyond was a sprawling garden full of greenery and colorful flora. All around, rising jagged and sharp, were the tall and spindly spires of Casamir's castle, caging me like the bars of a cell.

Above, the sky was blue but heavy with white clouds

that were so low, I felt as though I could reach and touch them.

It was truly beautiful here.

It had been a long while since I had looked upon anything and thought it was beautiful. It was a mark of how my life had changed, not because of Casamir or the five elven princes or even the toad in the well—all of that had been inevitable. My life had changed because I had come to know death at a young age, first when he took my mother and then when he took my sister and eventually my father.

Sometimes I would yell at him in the middle of the night.

You are selfish to have left me alone!

Ah, young one, he would reply. *It was not me who took your mother or your sister or your father. You killed your mother, you wished your sister dead, and your actions stole your father's last breath.*

He was not wrong, and when I questioned what I had done to deserve this loneliness, I remembered that I had made a terrible wish.

I hated that this place made me think of my family, and I ground my teeth against the feelings rising inside me, the strange cloudiness in my chest, the pinprick of tears in my eyes. I stepped out from the cover of the portico and into the garden.

A soft breeze caught my skirt, and it fluttered around me. I held on to handfuls of the flowy fabric to keep it from tangling in nearby brambles. As I wandered farther into the garden, it seemed to grow larger, full, taller, until it was all-consuming, and I could no longer see low-hanging clouds or even the pointed spires of

Casamir's castle. The path I had followed had long disappeared, overgrown with foliage, though it still remained before me. I wondered if this was Casamir's magic or the magic of the Enchanted Forest? Were they one and the same?

I knew little about magic except that it was cruel.

As I continued, I was careful not to touch anything or look too long at a beautiful flower for fear it would hypnotize me and lead me to some cruel fate. I might not have anything to live for, but I did not wish to die here among the fae. The path I was on led straight to a murky pond. It was surrounded by tall blades of grass and flowering trees, the petals of which were scattered across the surface of the water, which was dark in color and crowded with star-shaped blossoms, but none of that drew my attention like the naked man sitting at the center of the pond on a rock.

He was a selkie, a shape-shifting fae. Their natural form was that of a seal, and it was a skin they could shed so they could walk on land as a human. The sealskin was valuable, as it was the only way the fae could return to their true form and their true home, the sea.

This selkie was far from home and careless to my presence, sitting with his hands slightly behind him, head turned toward the sky, allowing the sun to bathe his bare body in golden light. His hair was brown, tousled by the wind, and his skin was bronzed, reddening more as each second passed beneath its rays. His muscles were hard, and so was his cock, which he made no effort to conceal.

He spoke in a singsong voice, and the words made my skin prick with unease.

"There is nothing more sweet than a maiden's call for me;
Body full of blood, a desperate heartbeat.
Warmed with lust, she comes to me frantic for release
And when that cloying death cry leaves her lips,
She breathes no more for me."

The words were a hypnotic spell, a weapon selkies used to lure their prey. I could feel it clouding my mind, and a strange lust tore straight down my chest like a knife, cutting me to the core. I fell to my knees, gnashing my teeth, digging frantically into the dirt and pressing the clay into my ears until the lyrics of the selkie's song were nothing more than a quiet mumble.

The lust dissipated and my body relaxed. I was disturbed by this creature's magic. I remained on my hands and knees feeling unsettled. For a split second, I had lost control of myself, and it had not been a choice. The realization shook my entire body, and I was struck by how this contrasted so violently with how I felt when I was near Casamir.

At least my reaction to him was genuine, no matter how much I hated it. I was attracted to Casamir, and that was all it took to desire him.

The selkie, though, was a predator.

My heart still pounded in my chest, frenzied from the fae's eerie song.

I gathered stones before rising to my feet, intending to use them as a weapon, but the selkie was no longer lounging on the rock. I scanned the pond for any sign of movement, but the water was still.

"Hmm, what do we have here?"

The voice came from behind me, and while it was

muted, I could still make out the words. I twisted too fast and fell, a scream bubbling up from my throat. As soon as I landed, the selkie straddled me. He had round eyes that seemed to shift from blue to green like the waves of the sea. His hair was wet, weighed down and dripping.

"Who are you, young maiden?" he asked.

I lifted my knee, shoving it hard into his balls. The creature fell onto the ground, and I found myself astride him, lifting my rock-filled hands over my head, readying to strike him in the face until his teeth were broken and he choked on his own blood, but then I noticed the skin of a seal lying near and snatched it from the ground.

I stumbled back with the selkie's skin in hand, and when he saw that I had it, his eyes grew wide.

"No, please! Give it back!"

I grinned and held one of the rocks to it.

The selkie need not know it wasn't sharp.

"Is this important to you?"

"You know it is important, you terrible thing!" he shrieked, spittle flying from his mouth. He managed to rise to his hands and knees.

"You are right," I said. "You cannot return to your true form without it, can you? What a shame it would be if it was cut to ribbons."

"What do you want, terrible thing? I will give you anything!"

It was the promise I sought, but before I could speak, something hit my cheek. The impact felt like a sting. I pressed my palm to my face and drew it away to find blood. My eyes shifted to find something floating before me—a small creature with wings, a sprite.

It was dressed in the petals of a pink rose that was spattered with my blood.

The sprite charged at my face, and I swatted at it, but suddenly there was a great swarm of them, and all I could do was cover my face as they cut and kicked and bit.

I stumbled back and fell into the pond with the sealskin still clutched in my hand, unwilling to let it go even as someone attempted to yank it away.

The jerk brought me to the surface of the water, where I came face-to-face with the selkie again.

"Whatever you want," he repeated, another promise. "Just give it back."

"If you are lying to me, I will stalk you for the rest of your life. You will never bask in the sun. You will never step on land without fearing me. I will hunt you until I flay you alive and burn this skin before your eyes. Do you understand?"

The selkie glared at me for a moment, and then his lips spread into a wide grin.

"I like you," he said. "I give you my word, terrible creature. I will give you your greatest desire."

I released his skin, and he hugged it to his body. I instantly regretted letting my one weapon go, but he did not slither away into his swamp like I had expected.

"Clean your ears, terrible thing," he said. "And tell me what you desire."

I watched him, mistrusting.

"Do you doubt my word, thing?" he asked, irritation flaring in his eyes.

I held my nose as I dropped below the murky water, twisting my finger into my ears to dislodge the mud. I resurfaced as quickly as I could, thinking that the selkie would flee, but once again, he proved true to his word and remained where he was in the water.

"There now," he said. "All better?"

"I need your prince's true name," I said.

"He is not my prince," said the selkie. "And that is not your greatest desire."

"You said you would give me what I desire," I said. "I desire to know the prince's true name."

"I said I would give you your greatest desire," he said. "There is a difference."

We stared at each other. I wanted to accuse the selkie of lying, but I realized this was my error. I had not been careful enough in the wording of our bargain. Did the selkie know what I truly desired, or could he merely sense that I was lying? Terror filled me as I realized I had unintentionally given him power over me.

"What do you call the prince?" I asked.

"We call him many names," he said. "The Thorn Prince, Prince of Thorns, Dreadful King, Shadow King. Some call him by his mortal name, Casamir, but those who do are very few."

"Why few?"

He shrugged. "A name precedes you, and without one, you are nothing."

"Then why go by a name that is not his own?"

"All fae go by names that are not theirs," he said. "True names are for lovers. True names are for death."

"Why only lovers and death?"

"A true name is a gift to the lover and a token to death."

"How do I find a true name?"

"The prince must tell you," he said.

"The prince will not tell me," I said.

That would mean he willingly set me free, and I doubted his generosity unless it involved frustrating me and an abundance of thorns.

"He will tell you if he loves you."

"You have lived too long in this swamp of a pond if you think the prince will ever love me."

The selkie grinned, chuckling under his breath.

"I do not believe you, terrible thing."

"I lost my ability to love a long time ago," I said. "I do not want it back."

"Perhaps you don't," he said. "And yet you still wish to be loved."

The blood drained from my face.

"I have no *desire* to discuss this," I hissed. "I need Casamir's true name."

The selkie studied me for a moment and then offered, "The mountains may know."

"The mountains?"

"The elven lords are old. It is likely no one knows their true name, save that which came before them—the earth and the Glass Mountains."

I frowned.

"The Glass Mountains are outside Prince Casamir's realm."

"So they are," said the selkie.

"I cannot go beyond the wall," I said.

Though I had said otherwise, I believed there were far worse creatures outside the his realm.

"Even if I managed it, I could not return in a day. He would notice I was gone."

And then what? I wondered.

Would the Enchanted Forest reprimand me? Or perhaps Casamir's five brothers?

"Perhaps you should fly," the selkie suggested unhelpfully.

"I cannot fly."

"Come back tomorrow," said the selkie. "And I will give you wings."

I hesitated.

"What would you ask for in return?"

"For now? Your smile," he said. "But one day when you rule this castle, you will return me to the sea."

CHAPTER SIX
Pity a Fool

I watched my creature leave the garden, her dress wet and clinging to her form like a second skin. There was a rage within me that the flowers and trees and the fairies and the selkie had seen her in such a state. My fingers curled into fists at my side.

"What are you sulking about?" Naeve demanded, hopping onto the bench beneath the window to peer out. When she saw my creature, she grinned wickedly, showing her crooked teeth. "Fancy her, eh?"

"I do not *fancy* her," I snapped, and yet I thought of how she must have gotten wet and knew the selkie had seen her. Had he seduced her with his horrible song?

"Is that why you begged her to speak your name?" Naeve asked.

The mirror choked, suppressing a laugh. I glared at the two.

"I *need* her to love me," I said again, just as I had last night, though I could not shake this feeling. It was sort of like dread, sort of like fear. What if she fell in love with someone else?

"And how will you make her love you?" asked Naeve. "She hates you."

I glowered. I knew that well enough, but perhaps with enough coaxing...

"Lust is not the same as love," said the mirror.

"I know the difference," I seethed.

The brownie raised a brow at me, and though the mirror had no expression, I knew it did the same.

"Who says she cannot lust for me and love me?"

Naeve exchanged a look with the mirror.

"Love is learned," said the mirror.

"You keep saying that, and yet no one has learned to love me," I said.

"And you have learned to love no one," said Naeve.

"She can learn to love me while she lusts," I said and turned back to the window, hating the disappointment that dropped into the pit of my stomach when I no longer saw my creature below.

"You will have to do more than fuck her if you want her to love you," said Naeve.

I spun to face her, no longer interested in the view.

"What do you know about love?"

The brownie glared back, a scowl on her face. "You expect true and devoted love from this woman, and yet you do not plan to give in return? What part about 'she hates you' do you not understand? You will have to woo her, and you have done a pitiful job of that thus far."

"She has been here for less than a day," I snapped.

"Precious time when you only have six days," said the brownie.

"Have you ever wooed anyone, Naeve?" I asked. She crossed her arms over her chest and lifted her brow at me. "And you, Mirror?"

His silence was telling.

"Then why would I listen to either of *you*?"

"The Mountains are trying to teach you a lesson," Naeve said.

I know! I wanted to scream so loud the Mountains would hear my rage, but I did not wish to give them the satisfaction of my frustration.

"What good is a lesson born from spite?"

"If you learn it, then it is revenge," said Naeve. "And you will know true love."

"True love," I snarled. "Who needs it?"

"You do, idiot," said Naeve, who jumped from her place on the bench and left my chamber. I had a feeling that if the mirror could leave, he would too.

"She is right, you know," said the mirror.

"No one asked you!"

"You posed the question. She answered it."

"It was hypothetical!" I yelled, throwing my hands in the air.

I started to pace. My body was tense, and I was frustrated. I had been frustrated since that creature had arrived in my room on her knees. This was her fault. I would not feel this way if she had never come. I would not have *hope*.

I hated hope.

I stopped pacing with my back to the mirror and began to ask, "How do I…"

I stopped abruptly.

This was ridiculous. I was an elven prince. Hundreds

of women had fallen in love with me. Why was this one different?

"Were you about to ask me how to woo a woman?"

"*No*," I snapped, folding my arms over my chest. I hated the embarrassment I felt and how it warmed my cheeks.

"I am a mirror."

"I *know* you are a mirror," I said. His meaning was twofold. He had never wooed a woman, and he also knew the truth behind my question. Yet I could not bring myself to ask it. "I know you watch my brothers."

"Your brothers are no more knowledgeable about love than you are," he said.

"Lore is in love," I said.

"With a mortal who does not know he exists," said the mirror.

"Cardic is charming," I said.

"Yes, and he uses his charms to bed women."

"But do they fall in love with him?"

"They usually end up hating him," said the mirror.

I frowned as I considered my other brothers, but none of them had managed to fall in love. Not even our father had loved our mother. Their union was one of convenience, and while they produced heirs, they had other lovers. Had they loved them?

"Perhaps you should ask someone who is actually in love," the mirror suggested. "Like the mortal prince you imprisoned for stealing a rose from your garden."

"I doubt he will help me."

The prince, whose name I did not know, had come from a mortal kingdom. He had hoped to scale the Glass Mountains and return to his kingdom with a golden apple, which grew inside the mountains. On his way, he stopped, climbed my walls, and plucked a flower from my earth for his princess. I kept him captive even after he begged to be set free to return to his betrothed.

"There's no harm in asking."

"There is always harm in asking."

Besides, I did not fancy being vulnerable to the mortal prince.

"It seems to me there is more harm if you do not."

"I hate you," I said, though I knew the mirror—and even Naeve—were right. I needed this woman to fall in love with me, and I was running out of time.

Which was how I found myself in the depths of my castle in search of the prince who had stolen a rose for his beloved. When I found him, he was resting on the stone floor, one knee drawn up. His head was turned to the window, which was shaped like half a moon and barred. Just on the other side, flower fairies had gathered to look upon him, but when they beheld me, they scattered in a flurry of wings and loose petals.

The prince turned his head lazily to me.

He had not been long in this world, his face youthful and full. He was as I expected all mortal prince's to be: flamboyant and arrogant. He had all the belief that the title he held outside the Enchanted Forest meant something to those of us who lived within.

But here, he was nothing but fuel to feed spells and fill stomachs.

He wore purple velvet and a hat that crushed his golden curls, and in the hat was a long, red feather.

"My captor arrives," he said.

"I hope you are not making bargains," I said. "The fae can be cruel."

"No crueler than you," he said.

"There is always someone crueler," I said.

The prince was quiet, so I spoke.

"Will you not beg me to set you free again?"

The prince smiled. "No, because that is what you want."

"It is not what I want," I said, frustrated that this mortal would even venture to guess my desires.

"Then what do you want?" he asked.

My eyes narrowed on the young prince, and I felt my body fill up with anger. He seemed to sense the danger, because he tensed.

"You are not to ask questions of me, mortal prince," I said. "I require your aid, and in exchange, I will grant your greatest desire."

"My greatest desire?" he repeated, his eyes gleaming.

"*Only* if your advice produces the results *I* desire," I added. I would set him free for nothing less.

"And what do you desire?" he asked.

I ground my teeth back and forth, not wishing to speak it aloud, but even as I stood here and thought about my true name, I had trouble recalling how it was spelled.

Seven letters, I reminded myself.

Your name knows no stranger.

Your name is the wail on the lips of a birthing mother.

Your name is the howl from the mouth of a grieving lover.

It is the cry that breaks the night when death is summoned.

"My desire is to make a maiden fall in love with me."

My nails cut into my palms as I waited for the prince to laugh, but all he said was, "She did not fall in love with you at first sight?"

"No," I gritted out.

She tried to bury an ax in my chest.

"Is that even real?" I asked.

"Of course it is," said the prince, who paused to think. "Perhaps she is not attracted to you."

"She *is* attracted to me," I snapped. I knew it. I could feel it in the air between us. The problem was that she also hated me.

The prince did not look so certain. I reached forward, wrapping my hands around the bars of his cell, and his eyes grew wide at the length of my claws.

"I asked you to tell me how to make her fall in love with me," I said. "Is your beloved princess not in love with you?"

"Of course she is," he said, as defensive as I felt.

"Then what made her love you?"

He thought for a moment and then said, "Have you told her she is beautiful?"

I blinked, slow.

"No."

"Well, is she beautiful?"

"Yes," I hissed.

She was more than beautiful, more beautiful than I cared to admit.

I thought of how she had looked at me upon her arrival, the shock that had come across her face, the fierceness that had taken over when she decided to fight me.

"Then you should tell her. All women want to hear they are beautiful."

I tried to imagine my creature melting into my arms at the sound of those words, but my mind only conjured an angry snarl.

"You are certain that will work?" I asked.

"If she does not fall in love with you immediately, it shall be a start."

My heart felt split in two. There was a side of it that rose with hope at the thought of having her love, and there was a side of it that felt completely ridiculous and would rather forget my name.

"If you are wrong," I warned, leaning closer so the prince could see my face between the bars of the cell. He paled and pressed against the stone wall, not as aloof as he appeared. "I shall cut the curls from your golden head."

With that, I left the prison to summon my creature.

CHAPTER SEVEN
The Fairy Ring

Once I returned to my room, I stripped off my wet clothes and opened the wardrobe only to have the door slam closed. I tried it again, and this time it wouldn't budge, as if it had been locked.

"Open this door!" I said as I pulled on the handle. "I need clothes!"

The door flew open, and I fell onto my back. A piece of cloth landed on my head. The door shut again, and I pulled the fabric off to find they had thrown a thin, sheer robe.

"This can hardly be considered clothes!" I yelled and shifted onto my knees, banging on the wardrobe, but there was no response from the creatures in the closet. I growled as I stood and slipped on the robe, laughing at its ridiculous coverage.

I crossed to the window and looked out, though the glass was mostly obscured by curling vines and golden-green trees. I could just make out the glistening peaks of the Glass Mountains, their jagged edges sitting on the horizon like ominous waves.

They were the mountains kings challenged suitors to scale, knowing no one ventured there and returned, and yet I was willing to go and learn the name of my captor—or at least attempt it—but dying out there was the same as dying here.

"I hate this place," I muttered, wrapping my arms around myself.

I turned to the bed and pulled back the covers, half-afraid I would find something slimy, courtesy of the pixies. While Casamir had fixed the broken window, I had no doubts they could find their way back in. But my sheets were clean, and I practically fell into the bed, curling onto my side.

For a few moments, I lay there, fighting tears stinging my eyes. At this point, I was not even certain what or who exactly I was crying for—my mother, my father, my sister, or myself.

Perhaps I only cried because everything in my life felt so unfair.

But the world did not care about fairness.

It rewarded those who already had, like Sheriff Roland, who believed he was entitled to anything and anyone as if it were his right by birth.

Casamir was no different, and I found myself at the mercy of both.

I buried my face in my pillow, eyes heavy, and drifted off to sleep, only to be woken suddenly by a loud knock at the door. Sitting up, I stared blankly at the door, heart hammering in my chest as the sound continued, rattling my bones. I felt as though I had just fallen asleep. My eyes were like jelly, and my body was damp with sweat.

"Yes?" I shouted groggily.

"Prince Casamir has summoned you," said the voice on the other side.

I did not recognize it as Naeve's raspy shout and did not respond. I groaned and fell back into bed, wondering what the prince would do if I did not come when he called.

Did I wish to find out?

I rose from the bed and knocked on the doors to the armoire.

"Hello?" I called. "I need to dress for dinner!"

There was no response.

I tried the doors but they still seemed to be locked. My knocking went unanswered.

Growling, I turned, catching my reflection in the now-darkened window. I would not leave this room dressed only in this robe, and I certainly wouldn't attend dinner with Casamir like this, not after the encounters I'd had with him since I arrived at his palace. So I returned to bed.

It did not take long for my eyes to grow heavy again, and just as sleep was about to take me, the door to my room burst open.

Casamir stood in the doorway, his dark and regal presence filling the room like night.

He was stunning.

Like all elven princes, I reminded myself, but there was something about this one. I had not felt so attracted to the others.

He was different, though I did not know why or

how. Perhaps it had something to do with his eyes, which were swallowed by pools of black, or his full lips, which were frustratingly pressed together. Whatever it was, my body *knew* when he was near and burned with a desire so keen, I found myself pressing my thighs together to suppress it.

"Did I not say come when I call?"

I narrowed my eyes. "Your creatures would not dress me."

"I do not care," he said, moving farther into the room until he stood at the foot of my bed menacingly, hands braced against the footboard. "Come as you are. Come when I call."

I glared at him and then shoved off my blankets and the bed, standing before him.

His eyes darkened as they roved over my body, veiled only in the shimmering, sheer robe his people had provided, and despite what he had said, I knew I would have seen something angry and possessive behind his eyes if I had shown up to dinner like this.

Without a word, he crossed to the wardrobe and beat on the door. When the fae answered, it was with a vicious expression until they saw Casamir, at which point they blanched.

"A gown for my guest. *Now.*"

They slammed the door and returned in seconds with a neatly folded swath of sparkling blue fabric.

As the elven prince took it, he commanded,

"Give her what she asks for or you will live no longer behind these doors."

The threat shook their tiny spines, and as the door shut, Casamir gave me the dress.

"Change."

I took it and stared.

"Will you stand and watch?"

"Why do you ask such questions when I have watched you bathe and dress before?"

"These are the actions of a lover, which you are not."

"I could be your lover," he said.

The comment was delivered so softly, it stunned me into silence. For a moment, I could only stare, and when I recovered, I cleared my throat and attempted a sharp reply.

"I would have to like you."

"Who says there must be like? There is passion and pleasure in hate."

I was not sure why it mattered to me, but somehow, I did not wish to give him the satisfaction of watching me. Perhaps I wanted it to feel like a punishment...like rejection. I turned from him and shed the robe, then stepped into the dress. As I slipped the sleeves on my shoulders, Casamir's hands were on the laces, pulling and tightening. I shivered as his fingers brushed against me.

The ease and intimacy of his actions burned my skin, and yet I did not dissuade him. I told myself it was because lacing my dress would be too difficult on my own and not because I had desired his touch from the moment he walked into the room.

"Do you help all your guests dress?" I asked, and while I managed to keep my voice light, I was surprised by how much jealousy wished to seep through.

"You are not a guest," he said.

I pondered asking him what he considered me—a prisoner, a curse, a thorn in his side—but kept quiet, and once he was finished tying the laces, I turned to face him. He offered his hand, and when I did not take it, his features grew hard.

"You have delayed my evening long enough," he said.

"What power you have given me," I said, amused.

He bared his teeth. "I am voracious," he said. "I shall feast tonight. Whether on food or on you, the choice is yours."

"I will hardly quell your appetite."

"Oh, sweet thing, I think you will."

The way he spoke was not lost on me, as if he and I were an inexorable truth.

I took his hand and let him lead me from my room, and as we passed into the hall that led to the portico, I could not help staying close to him to keep distance between me and the wall of thorned vines.

He glanced at me. "Afraid of my flowers?"

"Mistrusting," I corrected. "As with all things fae."

"But you are fae."

The urge to tell him to stop saying that clawed up my throat, but I did not speak, fearing if I did, he would torture me with those words.

We were quiet for only a beat, and then he spoke. "You spent time in my garden."

It was as if he were making an observation, and then I wondered if he had been watching me. Had he heard me speak with the selkie?

I glanced at him. "Is that a question?"

"Did you enjoy it?"

"Enjoy is not a word I would use to describe anything I have experienced here thus far."

I glanced at Casamir, noticing how his jaw popped as he ground his teeth.

"Why do I doubt you have enjoyed anything in your life thus far?"

I jerked my hand away from him and curled my fingers into fists as they hung at my sides.

We did not speak, and as we entered an unfamiliar part of Casamir's castle, I stayed one step behind, allowing him to lead. I hated how I now wished I had the warmth of his hand in mine. It was anchoring in this unfamiliar place, but I refused to reach for him and buried that want.

I needed no one.

Life had taught me that. Why else would it take away everyone who loved me?

We passed down a corridor, one side open to the night, and while I had watched it suspiciously before, I was suddenly distracted by the beauty of the vaulted ceiling, which was divided into sections by molding, detailed with vines and roses. The ceiling itself was painted blue, deep like the sky on a cold winter morning.

The hall opened into a dining room, which was dark, save for a few burning candles. A long banquet table ran down the center of the room, packed with tall candelabras, bouquets of weeping flowers, and platters of food. The smell of roasted goose curled into my nose and made my stomach roar with hunger.

"Where is your court?" I asked as Casamir made his way to the head of the table, noting that we were alone.

"Here and there," he answered as he sat. "Perhaps we will join them after you have eaten."

A trickle of unease shook my spine. I did not fancy an evening spent with tricky fae.

"Sit."

He indicated a spot beside him that was already set for me. I did so, though hesitantly, eyeing the food.

"Help yourself," he said.

I didn't, though my stomach gurgled loudly.

"There are rumors about fae food," I said. "Is it true if I eat here, I will remain in your realm forever?"

"The only way you will remain is if you do not guess my name," he said.

I watched him and he watched me. I wondered what he was looking for, wondered what I was looking for in him. Perhaps some sort of sign that I believed him. But my hunger won out and I filled my plate. The elven prince offered wine, which he poured into a gold chalice.

"Will you not eat?" I asked.

In answer, the prince plucked an apple from the cornucopia of fruit and bit into the crisp flesh. I watched his mouth as he ate, unable to keep myself from thinking about how his lips had skated across my skin.

"Pleased?" he asked.

Hardly.

I turned to my own food and chose a round globe grape to start. As I bit into the fruit, the juice burst from my mouth. I wiped it away with my fingers, sucking the stickiness from them.

When I glanced at Casamir, his mouth had hardened into a tight line, and his long nails had cut into the tender apple.

"Pleased?" I returned.

He narrowed his eyes and set the apple down. We

stared at one another, and then I focused on my food, conscious that he was watching my every move. I felt his eyes on me—on my hands as I reached for another grape, on my mouth as I bit into it, on my tongue as it darted out to clean my lips.

"What progress have you made toward discovering my name?" he asked.

"None save what you gave this morning, seven letters."

"The selkie gave you no direction?"

I did not wish to discuss what the selkie had given me, so instead, I asked, "Is the selkie a prisoner too?"

"I suppose that depends on what you consider a prisoner."

"Anyone here against their will."

"Then I suppose he is a prisoner."

"What did he do to incur your wrath?"

"He lured one of my own into his trap, so I lured him into a trap, and now he lives in my pond, where he sings and seduces the vulnerable and convinces them to set him free."

I did not speak, recalling the selkie's words.

One day when you rule this castle, you will return me to the sea.

"Will you visit him again?" he asked, the words light and careful. I got the sense that he had to work to control his voice.

"Yes," I said. "Tomorrow."

A strange tension built between us, a push and pull. I think the elven prince wished to know if the selkie had succeeded in seducing me, but I remained quiet and let him seethe in his uncertainty. What care should he have over who had touched me?

I was not his.

"You are beautiful," he said after a long moment of silence.

I was in the middle of biting into another grape when he spoke, and I froze at his words and their stiff sound. It was as if he were forcing himself to speak them.

"Excuse me?"

"I said you look beautiful."

His brows were low, his features tense, and yet he continued to hold my gaze as he spoke.

"Why do you seem so angry about it?"

"I'm not," he snapped. "I told you you were beautiful. Be grateful."

"Fuck you."

I took the goblet and tossed the contents at Casamir; the red wine dripped down his face like blood.

He stood so suddenly, the table quivered, and I flinched, pressing myself into my chair, which seemed to stun him. His eyes, which had filled with black, returned to normal.

"Who hurt you?" he asked and remained standing, fingers curled, as if he might leave the moment I answered his question.

"What do you mean?"

"There are bruises on your back. Who hurt you?" he asked again. "I need a name."

I was quiet for a moment, uncertain of what to say. It was not that I wanted to protect Roland. It was more that I did not wish to share my life with this prince. Still, Roland had chosen me to break the curse of the well, and he had done so believing he could pose as my rescuer.

I could make this go away. Marry me.

Even if he had not meant it, disgust twisted in my stomach at the thought of wedding the sheriff, at the thought of spending the rest of my life beneath him, bearing his children and his expectation that I would be an obedient wife.

Stranger still that he thought I would be what he wanted.

"I fell down a well," I said.

"Is that how my brother died?"

"I wish it were that simple," I said. If it were, I would not feel so guilty for what I did.

"What did you do?" he asked, his words whispered in the space between us.

"He guided me from the well, and I thought he would leave once he was free, but instead, he raced back toward it. I fought him, and in the struggle…he died."

I left out the part where I bashed his brains in, though I had no doubt Casamir knew.

"I was told I had to kill the toad in the well. It never occurred to me I could do anything else."

"Who told you to kill him?"

When I did not speak, he prompted, "Was it the man who threw you down the well?"

I met his gaze, and neither of us spoke.

"I will learn his name," Casamir promised. "And when I speak it, I will curse him to die a terrible death."

"Why would you do that?" I asked, confused by his concern.

"Because he hurt you," the prince said simply. Then he extended his hand. "Come."

I hesitated, my hunger hardly sated. Still, I pressed

my fingers into his, and he guided me from my seat toward another door on the opposite side of the dining room.

"Do you blame me?" I asked, unable to keep from doing so. "For your brother's death?"

"Yes," he said, and in the silence that followed, I felt guilt wash over me. "But you are asking the wrong question."

I eyed him. "What question should I ask?"

"If I care."

"Do your brothers care?"

"I imagine they do, or you would not be here."

He spoke apathetically, and rather than putting me at ease, it only made me angry. It would be easier to accept that I was a prisoner of someone who deeply loved the one they lost.

"Have you ever cared for anyone?"

I did not intend to sound so derisive, but I couldn't help it. If he could not stand up for those he loved, what did he stand for?

"I care for myself," he said. "I am all I need."

"Why am I not surprised?" I muttered.

If Casamir heard me, he did not speak. Instead, the doors before us opened to reveal his court and their unabashed revelry. The ballroom—at least I assumed that was where we were—looked more like a grove, ringed with trees, laden with glowing will-o'-the-wisps that cast a pale light on the crowd below. The number of fae in the room surprised me, considering I had seen so few through the day. But fae thrive beneath the stars, their antics fueled by the dark, and that was true of Casamir's court.

A cacophony of singing, deep laughter, and snickering jammed my ears, but the smell of fresh blossoms and sweet water was pleasant enough.

Fae of all types danced and drummed, dressed in the vibrant colors of new spring. My eyes moved from face to face, attempting to identify their kind, though my gaze caught on those who looked most like Casamir—tall, willowy elves who stared at me with contempt. They were all beautiful like him, cold like him, and they hated me...like him.

My heart had begun to race, and my hand tightened around Casamir's fingers.

"Do not fret, creature," he said and bent close, his breath hot against the shell of my ear. "No one will harm you...too much."

He pulled me into the fray without so much as a warning, and my hands were taken by two fairies with iridescent wings, one very tall and one very short. They dragged me into their dancing ring.

"Casamir!" I bellowed as the fairies jarred me one way and then the other.

Just this morning, he had begged me to say his name, and I had done so in a heady whisper, lured by his touch, drunk on the power it gave me. Right now, I screamed it with rage. I wanted to kill him, but my murderous thoughts were soon overtaken as I tried to keep my feet beneath me. I did not believe for a second the fae would stop their merrymaking if I fell. They would pummel my body until my blood covered their feet.

The fae moved fast, coiling through the grove, hand in hand, while others danced around us. I craned my neck this way and that, searching for any sign of Casamir, but it was almost as if he remained just out of sight—a shadow in my peripheral, a literal thorn in my side.

"She is looking for the prince!" one of the fairies shouted.

"She is in love!" another said, cackling viciously.

"I am not in love!" I snapped bitterly.

I was angry, and when I got my hands on him, he would pay.

The fairies broke from their line, and the tall one took both my hands. We spun, the weight of our bodies fully in our heels, and I thought that if she let go, I might fly into the sky. Hopefully when I landed, it would be on the Glass Mountains, I thought.

But the fae did not let go, and she pulled me back into a line, skipping as she went, and soon I felt my body relax into something more malleable. There was something provocative about the grove, about the smell of woodsmoke and the sweat beading off my skin and the pace at which we moved. My body grew damp, and a fire kindled deep in my belly. My face felt warm and flushed, my breasts heavy as arousal tore through me, as fierce and as violent as it had the night I met Casamir.

I was not sure how long I danced, but I knew that my feet hurt, and by morning, they would be covered in blisters. Part of me wanted to stop, part of me wanted to keep going, and part of me wanted to fuck.

Someone pushed me from behind, and I stumbled forward, hands planting on the bare chest of a fae with curly hair and the feet of a goat. He wore a halo of leaves that sat just behind two black horns that curled out of his head. He spun me and another fae took my hands, then another and another, until strong arms enveloped me and I looked up to find Casamir.

His face was warm in the glow of the fire, but his eyes were all black. His hands pressed into my back, my body bowing against the hard contours of him. In his embrace, the sounds of the grove fell away and the air grew thicker, heavier. My eyes lowered with the weight of it.

His hand came up to my cheek, and his thumb brushed my lips.

"Creature," he whispered, inclining his head as if to kiss me, but before his lips could touch mine, my legs gave way and I fell into a darkness as deep as the well.

CHAPTER EIGHT
The Glass Mountains

I woke up with a start and winced at the bright light streaming in from the window. Shielding my eyes, I sat up as last night's events reeled vividly through my mind. I did not know whether to be unashamed or embarrassed at how I had eventually played along, as fervent as the fae. It had not been wholly of my own will; the grove had its own magic, and it had seeped beneath my skin. I could still feel it clinging to my body.

I shoved off the blankets and discovered I was still dressed in last night's gown. At least Casamir had not undressed me, I thought. Though what would that have mattered? He had already seen me naked more than any man.

I moved to stand, and as I put weight on my feet, it felt as if they had been speared by a knife. I collapsed onto the bed again and lifted my foot to inspect my soles. They were red, swollen, and covered in blisters.

Fuck.

How was I supposed to meet the selkie today?

A growl of frustration left my mouth as I stood again. The pain was awful, and each step was like walking on needles. I should have guessed the consequences of dancing with the fae, should have known this would happen. I thought about how Casamir had thrown me into the fray, how he had remained out of sight until the very end.

I wondered now if he knew of my true plans with the selkie, if he had intentionally tried to sabotage me.

I held on to the bed until I came to the end of it and then hobbled across the floor, one slow step at a time, grinding my teeth until my jaw hurt.

I did not bother to change and slipped out the door, entering the hall, unable to use the wall for support as it was covered in poisonous flowers.

I made my way to the portico and sat, sliding down each step slowly. The relief it gave my feet was short-lived because soon I was standing again and making my way into Casamir's forest garden.

The dirt was no better on my feet, and I noticed that each footprint I made bore blood in the depressions, but still I continued. If anything, this horrible pain fueled my desire to make it to the Glass Mountains and learn Casamir's true name so I could be rid of this place.

Just when I felt as though I could not walk any farther, I saw the selkie ahead, perched on his rock, his curls a burnished crown beneath the sun.

I made my way to the bank of the pond and sat, shoving my throbbing feet into the cool mud.

The selkie raised his brow.

"Get caught in a fairy ring?"

My lip curled at his question. "Take me to the Glass Mountains," I said.

I saw no reason to make conversation. I had a bargain to win.

"I am afraid you will have to wait. Your escort grew hungry but will return."

I looked away from the selkie, over my shoulder, uneasy, and quickly looked back.

"Are you lying to me?"

"Are you accusing me of lying?" His eyes darkened, hinting at his fury.

"Who is this escort?"

"A trusted friend."

"There is no trust within these woods."

"He owes me a favor."

My shoulders tensed. I did not trust the selkie, and I would not trust him at all, even if his friend turned out to be real.

"Dip your feet into the water, terrible thing. It will soothe your soles...and your woes."

Again, I felt that dreadful sloshing in my stomach. I kept my feet in the mud and my knees pressed against my chest.

"How much do you know about Casamir?"

"So you are on a first-name basis?"

"He commanded it."

"And you listened?"

I glared at him. "You don't know anything about him, do you?"

The selkie narrowed his eyes.

"I know about him like we all know about him," he said. "But there is danger to speaking rumors as truth, especially in Fairyland."

Fairyland? Was that what they called this place?

"Then speak what you know as truth," I said.

His mouth was pressed into a hard line. "The prince is cursed like all his brothers. Some are cursed to despise, some are cursed to pine, but only one is cursed to die."

I considered the selkie's words and then asked, "Who cursed them?"

"Who didn't?" he countered, and his words made me angry, but I also knew that anything could become a curse if spoken close enough to magic.

"And you? What did you do to end up in the prince's pond?"

His jaw ticked, and I knew he did not like my prying question, but he answered.

"I lured a fair maiden to the edge of the sea, and she fell so deep in love with me, she died from longing. The fair maiden was a fairy queen, and when I left the safety of my sea, her people came for me. They stole my sealskin, and I wandered the land in search of it until I came to a cottage where a witch lived. I told her my woes, and she promised to help if I labored for her for seven years. So I did, and at the end, she offered a red-tipped thorn and said, 'Speak your wish to the thorn, and bury it beneath the full moon.'"

She gave no other instruction, and I did as she said.

"The next morning, I woke up beside my sealskin, which had grown from the ground. I had not felt such joy in seven years, but as I plucked it from the ground, the elven prince appeared—the one you call Casamir. 'Your sealskin belongs to me for it was made with my thorn,' he said. And I have lived in this pond since."

I remained silent following the selkie's story. It reminded me of the cruelty of the Enchanted Forest and

85

renewed my wish to escape my own looming imprison-
ment, not that I lacked desperation.

"And if you were set free? What would you do?"

"Return to my home," he said. "Return to what is left."

I squeezed my knees tighter to my chest as I thought
about what I would return home to—my empty cottage,
the full well, the geese who wandered in and out of the
Enchanted Forest.

There was nothing else, no one else.

"And what if there is nothing left?"

"Then I suppose I will die," he said.

A gurgling caw caught my attention, and I tilted
my head to the sky, finding a large black bird circling
overhead. He swooped down and landed near me, sweeping into a bow.

"Thing, meet Wolf the Raven."

"Wolf is an odd name for a bird."

"Thing is an odd name for a human."

"Thing is not my name," I said.

"Wolf is not my name," the raven said.

We stared at one another, and a smirk curled the
corner of my lips.

"It is nice to meet you, Wolf."

The raven's eyes glittered. "It is nice to meet you, Thing."

"Wolf will take you to the Glass Mountains," said the
selkie.

I looked from the selkie to Wolf. "How are you
going to take me to the Glass Mountains?"

"You will climb on my back, and I will fly you there."

"But I am far too large to ride on your back."

"Drink from the selkie's pond, and you will become
small."

I hesitated. "And when I return, will I drink again and return to normal?"

"What is normal?" asked the selkie.

I glared, and he answered, "Yes, you have my word."

His word was binding, so I knelt by the pond, dipped my hands into the water, and drank.

I stood to my full height and then felt the world grow larger and larger around me. The pond was now a vast ocean, the flora now a dark and deep forest, and the raven a monster. My feet did not hurt, and when I lifted my foot, I found that they had healed.

"Now then," said Wolf as he bowed. "Climb, Thing."

My fingers sank into his feathers, and I gripped them as I clambered onto his back.

"Hold tight!" he said, stretching his large wings and lifting off the ground.

The beat of his wings was loud, and the wind felt like a physical thing, cutting across my face as we ascended into the air and took off toward the mountains, which I could see in the distance now that I was above Casamir's castle. There wasn't much I feared, perhaps because I was not afraid of death, but seeing the mountains in all their splendor made me afraid.

They curtained the horizon, glittering in bright, blinding flashes of light. Their brilliance was almost too much to behold, but I squinted against the splendor, making out their sharp, needlelike peaks and harsh edges, realizing that without the sun, the mountains were nothing save slabs of cold rock.

Though that did nothing to lessen the dread boiling in the pit of my stomach.

I peeked at the world beneath my feet, which was thick with forest and cut through by streams, but my eyes held on the rounded green and gold roofs of what looked like a palace.

"Who lives below?" I asked the raven, though I was not certain he could hear me.

"That is the Kingdom of Nightshade. It is ruled by one of the seven."

"One of Casamir's brothers?"

"The third one, Prince Lore."

Lore. I remembered him, the one who had taken my knife.

What kingdom had the dead brother ruled? Who ruled it now?

"If there are seven princes, is there a king?"

"The Elder King is dead."

"And he left no heir?"

"He left seven."

"That is not what I mean. Why are there still seven princes? Why is there no king?"

"The king could not choose between his sons, so he declared upon his death that whoever reassembled the Magic Mirror shall be king of the Enchanted Forest. One piece to each brother and there has been no king since."

"That seems like a horrible way to choose a king," I said.

Though having met all seven princes, I was certain the king recognized that none of his sons would make suitable kings.

"Or perhaps it is a perfect way," said Wolf.

The raven continued to glide through the air until he soared over the Glass Mountains, and then he began to circle and descend.

I shielded my eyes as the sun reflected off the surface of the mountains and watched in wonder as we landed on a slope between crests that rose like great pillars and kissed the sky.

"Off, Thing," said Wolf, and I shifted my leg over his back and slid off the raven's back.

My feet slipped as I hit the ground, but I steadied myself before I could fall. Still, my legs felt fragile and shook with my weight after my flight through the sky.

"What do I do?" I asked Wolf.

"Knock," he said.

Gingerly, I bent and rapped my knuckles against the smooth surface of the mountain and was surprised by how the sound echoed around me, vibrating the air, but then silence fell like a shroud, pressing against my body like a heavy weight.

"Hello?" I called as I stood.

"Speak!" Wolf commanded. "The mountains are listening."

I watched the raven for a moment, hesitating, feeling silly only speaking to the wind.

"I've come to learn the true name of the Prince of Thorns," I said.

Wolf and I stood in the silence again, and as it blanketed us, I scanned the glistening slopes of the mountains as if someone or something might appear at any moment and eat me alive.

But then the mountain spoke, and it was as if its voice were inside my head. The sound resonated, rumbling throughout my body.

"What will you give me in exchange?" the mountain asked.

My heart beat harder in my chest.

"What do you want?"

The mountain paused and then spoke, "Bring me three hairs from the head of the Prince of Thorns, and I will tell you his true name."

Then the weight that had fallen on me when we

landed dissipated. My body slumped, no longer on edge, and I could breathe once more.

I turned to the raven, expecting something more.

"Come, Thing. We must return."

Climbing onto the raven's back was harder with the slippery floor beneath me, and I yanked on his feathers as I mounted him. Wolf squawked in pain, but once I was seated, he took flight. I stared down at my hands, tangled with Wolf's feathers, reminding me of Casamir's thorns. My vision blurred, mind whirling with ways to secure three of Casamir's hairs.

Perhaps I could sneak into his room while he slept and pluck them from his head, but where did he sleep in his vast castle? I thought I had been there once, when I first arrived, but his castle was like an endless forest and felt impossible to navigate.

Though I should not care, I wondered what the mountains wanted with his hair. Worse, what if I gave it and received the wrong name?

I tried to recall the exact words I had used when I had told the mountains what I wanted but could not remember.

"Why would the mountains ask for Casamir's hair? And only three strands?"

"It is not for me to wonder," said Wolf, whose help, I realized, only extended to his wings, which I supposed was enough.

The selkie still lounged on the rock, and when we landed, he straightened.

"Well, do you have a name?" he asked in a bored tone.

"I have a task," I said. "But you knew that."

"Nothing in this world is free," said the selkie.

I looked at Wolf. "Thank you."

I was sincere, grateful that the bird had not tried to trick me or leave me on the mountains. Though, I was far more suspicious that he hadn't done anything at all.

He swept into a bow, one wing to his breast. "My pleasure, Lady Thing."

"I am not—"

But the raven sprang into the air and flew away before I could finish, and I was left with the selkie, who gestured to the water.

"Drink," he said. "And you will grow big again."

The pond was a vast ocean, and my feet sank into the mud as I neared the bank, but I scooped the water into my hands and sipped. As soon as it touched my tongue, my head spun and my world was righted once more.

My stomach revolted, and before I could stop myself, I bent and vomited into the grassy bank.

"Tsk, tsk, tsk," he said. "The fairies will not like that."

I spit, trying to remove as much of the sour taste from my mouth as possible, and wiped my mouth with the back of my head, glaring at the selkie.

"Why?"

"They are not fond of anyone who mucks up their space."

"What was I supposed to do? Swallow it?"

"That would have been better than what they will likely plan for you."

My stomach churned with dread at his words, but I turned and left the pond.

CHAPTER NINE
A Good Bargain

I had seethed all night, my body simmering with rage and lust, both warring for a foothold inside me as I replayed my time with my creature. She had rejected my compliment and insulted my hospitality. All of that I might have punished had she not flinched when I stood.

It took the anger out of me as fast as it had swallowed my eyes.

"She expected me to hurt her," I said.

"You did hurt her," said the mirror. "You held her down with your thorns, and you let the red caps throw stones, and last night you let the fae dance with her until her feet bled."

I rose into a sitting position where I sprawled on my bed. "She fled," I said about the first. "As for the second, I gave her a choice, and the third…that was a mercy. She said she would visit the selkie again."

"Did you try talking to her about the selkie?" asked the mirror.

I crossed my arms over my chest. "*You* try talking to her. She's impossible!"

"She cannot be any worse than you."

"When I told her she was beautiful, she threw wine in my face," I said.

A garbled sound escaped the mirror.

I glared, and it turned into a choke, as if he were swallowing the laugh.

"How did you tell her?" he asked.

"What do you mean, how did I tell her? I said, 'You are beautiful.'"

"And...?" he prompted.

"She was confused," I admitted. "And then I told her she should be grateful for my compliment, and she was not."

There was tension in the silence that followed, and then the mirror said, "You are an idiot."

I slid off the bed and stalked toward him. "Careful, you glorified piece of rock."

"Do you think the creature is beautiful?" he asked.

"Of course I think she's beautiful," I snapped. "As if my raging erection wasn't evidence enough!"

"Then why don't you tell her again," he suggested. "And this time, mean it."

"I did mean it!"

"There is a time for these things," said the mirror. "Perhaps *after* she has softened toward you."

"You must be forgetting the part where I need her to fall in love with me."

"She will not fall in love with someone she does not know, and all you've managed to show her is how much of an ass you truly are."

"I am not an ass!"

I glared at the mirror, and he glared back—or rather, it *felt* like a glare—and after a moment, I let out a breath and fell against the bed.

"Okay, fine. I'm an ass."

I stared at my ceiling, which was covered in layers of fabric that draped around my bed like a heavy cloak in winter.

"Perhaps you could...take her on a picnic," the mirror suggested. "You could...take her to a favorite place and...*talk*."

A laugh tore from my throat. "That is a ridiculous idea. She will hardly speak to me at dinner. What makes you think she would follow me into the forest for a *chat*?"

"It was only one suggestion," said the mirror. "Maybe you could—"

"I'll ask the prince again," I said, interrupting him.

"You would give him another chance?"

I noted the surprise in his voice.

"Not without consequence," I said. "I have five days left. No more. I cannot afford to waste time!"

"Of course not," said the mirror. "You must be on your way. Hurry before it is too late."

His voice dripped with contempt, and if he had not made me so angry, perhaps I would have inquired after his tone.

Instead, I started to leave.

"Do you even know where she is?" the mirror asked.

I paused at the door and looked over my shoulder. From this distance, I could see my reflection.

"Likely in her room," I said. "She cannot walk."

When he said nothing, I turned fully toward him.

"Why?"

"No reason," he said airily. "But if I wished to woo a woman, my day would start and end with her."

I ground my teeth.

"What do you know? You are just a mirror!" I slammed the door behind me, but as I made my way to the dungeon, my steps faltered, the mirror's words worming their way into my brain.

Where is she?

Fucking mirror.

I abandoned my task for my creature's room. When I arrived, I knocked and gave her no time to answer before I entered, too impatient to know if she was there.

She wasn't.

The room was empty, the bed was made, and the sheer robe she'd worn the night before lay in a puddle at the foot of her bed. I crossed the room to pick it up. The thin material was almost as light as air, and when she'd stood from her bed dressed in only this, I had lost any hold I'd had on my anger and spent the entire evening and night attempting to quell my impossible arousal.

I should have taken her then. I could have. She would have bent to my will with just as much enthusiasm, and yet I could not bring myself to close the distance between us because I knew in the aftermath, she would hate me and I would despise myself.

I pressed the robe to my face and inhaled her sweet, rosy scent.

"What are you doing?" My creature's voice was sharp and demanding.

I turned, robe in hand, to look at her.

She was still dressed in last night's clothing, her hair

windswept and wild, and her bright eyes narrowed. But her features lacked the tightness of anger. Perhaps she was too tired to hold on to those feelings, as a darkness gathered beneath her eyes.

She may have slept last night, but it certainly wasn't restful.

"Where have you been?" I asked.

A light ignited in her eyes, and it pulled at the corners of my mouth. There was her fury.

"I told you yesterday I would visit the selkie."

"You returned?" I blanched. "With those feet?"

"Of course with my feet," she snapped. "Whose would I have used?"

I dropped the robe and stalked toward her. "I warned you against returning."

She smiled wickedly. "Did you really think a fairy ring would keep me from learning your name?"

"Is that what you are doing?" I asked, stopping within an inch of her. She shifted, straightening her shoulders, curving her back. She was preparing to fight me, and I wondered if she knew it. I leaned in a centimeter more and demanded, "Did you bargain with the selkie?"

"So what if I did?" she asked.

I reached for her, my hand bracketing her neck where her pulse raced against my palm.

"Do not toy with me, vicious creature," I said, voice quiet. "Tell me truthfully, did you bargain with the selkie for my name?"

She must have seen something in my eyes that hinted at my anger, because I felt the fight leave her body.

"No," she whispered.

"And will you promise never to do so?"

"No."

I narrowed my eyes. "I can give you everything he could and more."

"There is nothing I want from you except freedom," she said, but as she spoke, her eyes fell to my lips.

I leaned closer, a whisper between our mouths. "Are you certain of that, creature?"

When she did not speak, I lost all control and crushed my mouth to hers. For a brief moment, she tensed, but as my tongue swept over her lips, she melted, her mouth moving just as hungrily as my own.

I could not decide where to put my hands. What would she want? I'd had no issue touching her before, but this felt precarious. The wrong move could end it too soon, and I wanted this for as long as possible. But it was she who fueled the fire when her arms wound around my neck to bring me closer. Her breasts pressed against my chest, her mouth opened for me, and her tongue caressed mine.

Fuck, she was sweet.

My hands went to her waist and then to her thighs, and I lifted her off her feet. Her legs encircled my waist, and I pressed my weight into her as her back met the door of her wardrobe. My cock was so hard and so heavy, and as it found friction between her thighs, I groaned and she gasped, her fingers tightening in my hair.

I sought purchase against the naked skin of her thighs, my palm resting against her wet heat, my fingers trailing the slickness gathered there.

"Sweet creature, say you are desperate for me."

"Do not speak," she begged. "I will hate you more."

She pulled on my hair and pressed her mouth harder to mine. I froze, reaching for her hands and pinning them against the door.

We glared at one another, breathing hard.

"Vicious creature," I said.

"Beast," she spat.

In retaliation, I ground into her, smiling wickedly when her head fell back against the door, exposing the creamy column of her neck to my mouth. I sucked on her skin until a cry tore from her throat.

"Deny yourself my pleasure, creature," I said, lips trailing her jaw. "It will only drive you mad."

I met her gaze but did not kiss her again. She glared back, her skin flushed, her lips swollen.

"Let. Go."

Her demand twisted throughout my body, frustrating every limb, but I obeyed and lowered her to the ground. I could not bring myself to give her distance, and she did not push me away. Instead, her eyes lowered to where my arousal strained against the front of my tunic before she stepped into me, her head tilted back to hold my stare.

"Give me a letter," she said, her breath caressing my lips. "And I will relieve you of this misery."

Her words made my body ache, and I twined my fingers into her hair, claws grazing her scalp. She barely winced. I wanted to refuse her, but I was desperate and lust-filled, and I did not think I could continue with this pounding in my head, heart, and cock.

"U," I said.

"Me?" she asked, a line appearing between her brows.

"U," I said again. "The letter."

There was a breath of silence before my hand tightened in her hair.

"On your knees," I said, and she lowered to one, then the other, gaze unwavering.

I lifted my tunic and reached into my pants to pull out my heavy cock, red in color from the amount of blood rushing to the head. I watched my creature as she looked at it. Her eyes widened, but she took it into her hands and licked me from base to tip. As her tongue and mouth closed over the crown, my hands returned to her hair, gathering it from her face so I could watch her taste me.

She kept her hand on me, a steady pressure that worked up and down my shaft, and now and then, she would look up to watch my face as if she truly cared for my pleasure. I leaned into it, begging, hoping, *wishing*.

"Fuck."

The word slipped between my teeth as I lost myself in her soft, warm, and wet mouth. She was perfection at my feet, and I closed my eyes as my body tightened and a tingling feeling consumed me as I came, a raw sound escaping my mouth as she sucked me hard before letting me go. I took her face between my hands as I stared at her, flush and rosy and fucking beautiful.

"You are a sweet creature," I said, and she rose to her feet and pulled me against her, her mouth colliding with mine. I could taste my come in her mouth as her tongue thrust against mine.

I gripped her tight, but she pushed me away.

"A letter," she said. "For each time you wish to come by my hand."

I narrowed my eyes, a strange mix of emotions warring inside me. The futile hope I'd had that she might like me in some small way as she'd taken me into her mouth vanished.

"You presume much, creature."

"Tell me when your cock is in my mouth again," she said.

We were only inches apart, and I leaned closer to her, speaking in a half whisper.

"Do not act as if you are not wet for me, vicious creature," I said, a clawed finger trailing down her face. "I touched you. I *know* you."

She shoved against me, but I did not move.

"Leave!" she commanded, breathing hard, fists clenched.

I studied her, unable to keep my mind from imagining what it would be like to take her sweet center against my mouth. My once-softened cock hardened at the thought.

"As you desire," I said, but I paused at the door after restoring my appearance. When I looked over my shoulder at her, she was staring at the opposite wall, her profile tense and angry, and her mood only darkened as I spoke.

"Come when I call, sweet creature," I said. "Or I will come for you."

CHAPTER TEN

Three Strands of Hair

I pressed my fingers to my lips in quiet disbelief of what I had done, what I had *wanted* to do to the elven prince. I had not expected him to kiss me, and when he did, I had been powerless to resist because I hadn't wanted to. This whole time, I'd been afraid that he would eat me whole, and here I'd desperately wanted it.

It was a means to an end, I told myself. Anything to make myself feel better about the fact that I had willingly taken the prince's cock into my mouth.

I could still taste him on my tongue.

I could still smell the warmth of his skin.

I could still feel the sharp tug of his hand in my hair.

And I would gladly take more.

Fuck me.

I knelt and plucked one dark hair after another from my floor until I had three long, black strands sitting in my palm. Carefully, I twisted them around my finger and knocked on the doors of my wardrobe. Unlike last time, it opened a crack, though I could not see who answered.

"I need a pouch...a small one to keep something safe," I said.

The door shut quietly, and after a moment, the fae in the armoire produced a small square of fabric that closed with two golden ties. I took it, and before I could say anything, the door shut again. I slipped the hairs inside, pulling the strings tight, and shoved it between my breasts to keep it safe as I made my return to the selkie's pond.

My journey was easier now that my feet were healed, though my mind wandered to Casamir and the intimacy we had shared, and the more I thought about it, the more I ached. A desperation took root in the bottom of my stomach, and by the time the pond came into view, my mind had conjured images of me and the elven prince locked together and writhing.

I had to get out of here before I did something I regretted.

A feeling of unease shivered down my spine, just as it had when I had visited before. My steps slowed and the feeling continued, raising the hair on the nape of my neck. I turned my head slowly, peering into the flora around me, but saw nothing of note.

It is probably fairies playing tricks on you. I thought of the selkie's parting words, but my heart continued to race, and I felt an overwhelming sense of dread as I faced the pond.

"You've returned."

The voice startled me, and I whipped around to face the selkie, who stood in his human form. He was naked, his burnished body on display. I let my eyes descend over his hard muscles, unnerved by his erection, but I was seeking his weakness, the sealskin, which was not near.

"Can you call for Wolf?" I asked.

The selkie took a step toward me, and I took one back.

"So you have succeeded? You have three hairs from the prince's head?"

As he spoke, he continued his approach, as sly and stealthy as a jungle animal. I felt cornered as the back of my feet sank into the muddy bank of the pond.

His eyes narrowed on my neck. I did not know what he saw, but I could guess. Casamir had sucked my skin hard into his mouth.

"You bear his mark."

I covered my skin where it was most sensitive and narrowed my eyes.

"I did not tell you about the three hairs," I said.

And then the selkie launched himself at me. I barely had time to move before he crashed into me. I hit the water so hard, it stole my breath. As I sank beneath the surface, my chest was crushed under his weight. I struggled to be free even as my mouth filled with water and my lungs burned.

He held me down until I thought I would die and then dragged me to the surface.

"Where are they?" he demanded. Gripping me by my upper arms, he shook me. "Give them to me!"

I could not speak, too desperate for air.

The selkie dragged me up his rock at the center of his pond and held my legs down with his powerful thighs so I could not kick. I still fought, clawing at his hands, which drove into my pockets. When he did not find the hairs, he squeezed my breasts. I pulled his hair and jabbed at his eyes, but his hands clamped down on my wrists. Once he had them secure, he groped me and then ripped the bodice of my dress, smirking as he lifted the pouch.

"Foolish thing," he said, and his fingers closed over the bag as he forced his mouth on mine.

"No!" I screamed. "Wolf! Casamir!"

"Shut up!" the selkie said, and he placed his large hand over my nose and mouth, pressing down until I could not breathe. I dragged my nails down his arms, and I knew that I broke skin because I could feel it beneath my nails. Yet he did not loosen his hold, and just when my vision began to blur, a shadow passed over us from above. In the next second, Wolf swooped down and began to claw at the selkie's face with his feet and peck at his eyes with his sharp beak.

The selkie screamed as blood dripped down his face, and he dropped the pouch he had stolen from me. I raced to snatch it up and slipped off the rock, wading through the water as fast as I could.

"Drink, creature, drink!" Wolf commanded, but I could already feel myself growing smaller and smaller and the pond larger and larger. The bigger it grew, the farther away from shore I was and the more exhausted I became. And just when I thought I could go no farther, the raven swept me from the pond with his taloned feet.

I shook uncontrollably as a numbness took hold inside me. I felt nothing, not even the wind on my face.

"Are you all right, creature?" Wolf asked, but I did not answer because I didn't know what to say. I was not all right, but I had a purpose and I needed to see that through. I was too close to freedom.

I kept my eyes closed the entire flight, and when Wolf landed, he set me gently on the cold, glass surface of the same clearing and landed nearby. I rose dizzily into a sitting position, watching him.

"Why did you save me?" I asked.

"Because you will marry the prince," said Wolf. "And when you do, I shall be a wolf once more."

The selkie had said something similar. I had not believed him then and I did not believe Wolf now, but I said nothing as I stood, untying the pouch and pulling out Casamir's dark hair. It was wet and stuck to my fingers, but I managed to count each strand to ensure all three were there.

"Mountains," I said. "I have brought you three strands of hair from the head of the Prince of Thorns."

After I spoke, the world seemed to go still and silent, the pressure of it pushing against my ears. Then the ground beneath me groaned and a hole opened up at my feet.

"Feed me, mortal."

"You promise to give me the prince's true name?" I asked.

The hole grew bigger, touching the tips of my toes, and I jumped back to keep from falling in.

"Feed me, mortal!"

My chest tightened, but I obeyed. I thought I had been careful in the way I'd worded my bargain with the mountains, but I could not remember the exact wording. Still, we had made a bargain, and I had no reason to believe the mountains would not honor it. I let

Casamir's hair drop into the darkness below, and the hole closed with a snap, but then the ground began to shake. It was different from before—not the grumble of a voice but a tremor of anger.

"You think you can trick me, mortal?" the mountains roared in my head, making my ears ring. I fell to my knees and pressed my palms flat against them.

"It's not a trick!" I seethed. "The hair came from his head!"

"Liar!" the mountains bellowed. "Only one hair came from his head. The others did not, and now you must pay for your deceit!"

A smaller hole opened up before me, and the hands that were pressed against my ears were suddenly flush against the surface of the Glass Mountains.

"Only your flesh will suffice," said the mountains, and as they spoke, my ring finger dropped into the opening of the mountain against my will. Just as before when it closed to swallow the hair, it closed to swallow my finger, slicing through skin and bone.

The pain was sudden and sharp, stealing my breath for only a beat before a scream tore from somewhere deep in my throat. I ripped my hand away and cradled it in the other, blood dripping through my fingers and striking the ground.

I looked at Wolf, who still watched nearby.

"Come, Lady Thing," he said and nothing more.

My face was hot with shame, made worse with the knowledge that someone had witnessed my failure. My eyes fell to my hand, and I wrapped it in the skirt of my dress before rising to my feet. The raven was gracious and bowed low so I could mount his back. While he flew, I did my best to keep the emotions mixing in my chest at a distance, but they raged, threatening and volatile.

When we were within view of the pond, I knew I was in trouble because Casamir waited at the edge of the water. He was a dark and foreboding figure, haloed in black thorns and shadow. In one hand, he held the selkie's sealskin. In the other, he held the selkie's severed head.

Wolf croaked, circling once before landing on the bank near Casamir's feet. I tipped my head up at him, a giant from where I stood, and slid off Wolf's back. As I took a drink from the pond and grew, the raven bowed to the prince, but Casamir did not seem at all concerned with the raven. His eyes did not move from mine.

"How did you know?" I asked after I had grown tall.

"You called and I came," he said.

Neither of us spoke for a moment, and then all of a sudden, I rested my head against his chest and burst into tears.

CHAPTER ELEVEN
A Daring Rescue

I did not know what to do when my creature placed her head against my chest and began to cry, but her tears were like knives, tearing at my heart, feeding a desire to avenge her pain. I was not used to these feelings, mine or hers.

Bewildered, I looked at the raven, who circled his wings before him.

"What?" I mouthed.

The raven stretched his wings and repeated the movement.

I shrugged, confused.

"Comfort her, you idiot!" the raven said in a half whisper.

I let my magic recede and dropped the selkie's head to place my arm around her, but before I could, she pushed away.

"I hate this place," she said, glaring at me. I felt the full force of her fury as if she had slapped me. "I hate *you*."

"I told you not to return," I said. My body grew hot, my hands tightening in the selkie's sealskin. She had no right to rage at me. She was here because she killed my brother, and she was here now because she had ignored my warning. "I told you he was dangerous."

"As if you are any better," she spat.

"Oh, vicious creature, you do not want me to *be* better. I am the only thing that can protect you here."

Her gaze fell to the sealskin in my hand, and then her eyes shifted to the selkie's head, which looked up at her from the ground.

Her eyes still glistened with unshed tears, like emeralds shining in the earth. I hated that I had missed the chance to take her into my arms. No doubt I would hear about it later from the mirror, who was likely watching this exchange with Naeve.

The raven was right. I was an idiot.

And now she hated me, though I supposed she'd never stopped.

I studied her, noticing the blood on her dress.

"Are you hurt?" I asked, uncertain if she had just brushed against the selkie's bloodied head, but then I noticed how she held her hand in her dress. I took a step forward, discarding the selkie's skin. "Let me see your hand."

"I'm fine," she said, taking a step back.

"Let me see it," I said, the words slow and deliberate. Something in my voice must have convinced her to obey because she lifted her bloodied hand to show her missing finger. "Where is it? Your finger?"

"The mountains took it," she said.

"The mountains have your blood?"

"I could not resist," she said.

"Because you bargained with them," I seethed. "Foolish creature! What did you trade?"

She was quiet.

"*Creature*," I warned, the word slipping between my teeth.

She did not look at me as she answered. "Three strands of your hair."

"Three strands?"

Her gaze met mine. "I only had one. The other two must have belonged to your mistress."

"Or a *brother*," I snapped.

Her mouth tightened. "This is your fault! I would not have traded anything if I had not wished to guess your true name!"

"No one told you to bargain with the mountains!"

"He did!" she said, pointing to the selkie's head.

"He wanted to kill me!" I yelled, kicking the head, sending it soaring into the surrounding woods. "I would have given you my name had you sucked my cock for four more days!"

It did not matter that I did not have the time. It did not matter that she must love me too.

"If I desired you the least bit, I might consider another trade, but as it is, you are the last person in this forsaken place I would ever fuck!"

"Do not be so certain, especially where your freedom is concerned."

"Do not degrade me for giving you pleasure."

"I am not degrading you," I said. I felt myself bending over her, but she was just as stubborn, rising on her toes to match my venom. "If you let me, I would *worship* you. Perhaps then you might know what it is to be grateful."

She slapped me and I reeled back, pressing a hand to my face to quell the sting, though it was covered in the selkie's blood.

Her eyes glistened as she stared back at me, and I could not figure out what I had said that had made her angrier.

"Do not make me feel worse for something I already regret."

I felt like she had cracked open my chest and laid everything inside me bare, and I hated it.

"If you had told me why you wanted my hair, I could have saved you a limb. The mountain does not know my name."

"I am beginning to think no one knows your name. Perhaps you have no name at all."

"I have many names," I said. "It is the consequence of living so long."

"A cruel existence," she seethed. "Perhaps you should die, and you would not have so many."

"Ah, but they do not end when you die," he said. "I have died many times and I will come back with more."

She paled at my statement, and I inched closer to her.

"Give me your hand," I said.

She hesitated but stretched her arm out, trembling.

I took her hand and placed her injured finger in my mouth. Just as I predicted, she tried to pull away, but I held her, sucking hard, and when I released her, her flesh and bone were restored.

Her eyes widened with amazement for one second and then darkened with horror.

"No! I did not ask this of you!"

"You did not," I affirmed.

"T-take it back!" she said, holding her hand aloft as if it did not belong to her.

"I will not," I said.

"I do not want to owe you for this. *Take it back!*"

"Did I ask for anything in exchange?"

"It does not matter that you didn't," she said. "Magic always requires a trade."

"Then let me worry about what it will want," I said and bent to pick up the sealskin. I stepped around her just as the selkie's head rolled out from the surrounding flora, pushed by a tearful winged fairy.

"Do not cry for such a creature," I said. "He touched what is mine."

I snatched the head from the ground by his golden hair.

When I turned to my creature again, she was staring at the selkie's head.

"What are you going to do with that?"

"I will plant it outside my window and watch what grows," I said.

She said nothing, and she did not ask me what I intended to do with the sealskin either, but if she had, I likely would have told her about my collection of skins, which ranged from animal to human. One never knew when they might need a different skin.

"Come, we must go," I said. "Dusk is approaching fast."

She raised a brow. "Are you afraid of the dark?"

"No," I said. "But you should be, even when I am near."

I spoke only once on our return and that was to instruct my creature to walk a step ahead of me so that I may watch her from all sides. When we came to the palace, I threw the selkie's head into the center of the courtyard and then looked at her.

"The mountains have your blood now," I said. "They will call to you, and when they do, you must resist."

"How will I know if they call?"

"It is likely you won't."

She narrowed her eyes. "You are *most* unhelpful."

I smiled, half-hearted, only amused by her frustration. "Do not leave your room tonight, no matter what calls."

Her throat constricted as she swallowed, and my eyes dropped to the mark I'd left on her skin. I reached across our distance and touched her there. I wanted to kiss her, to lick her, to suck her skin again, but she winced, so I let my hand fall away.

"Good night, creature," I said, and she fled.

I returned to my chamber and dodged a shoe as I entered.

"What the fuck was that for?" I asked, glaring at Naeve, who stood on the bench beneath the window, hopping on one leg as she tried to take off the other shoe.

"Because you are an idiot! A royal one!" she yelled.

"What did I do this time?" I demanded.

Her answer was to launch another shoe at me, and I brought my arm up in time to block my face.

"*You should be grateful?*" Naeve said, quoting me. "Could you be any less romantic?"

"That is not what I meant!"

I meant that she might understand how grateful I had been when she'd knelt before me and took a part of me into her mouth, and I was desperate to return the favor.

Naeve searched for something else to hurl at me.

"What else was I supposed to say?"

"Anything else! Anything *kind*!" she said. "If she is going to love you, she has to like you, and there is nothing about you that is remotely likable."

She plucked a pillow from behind her and pitched it at me.

"Stop throwing things!"

"You have five days! *Five*!"

"I can count!"

"Then make them count!"

"I'm *trying*!" I yelled. "Do you imagine this is somehow easy when I have had no love in my life?"

Naeve froze, the candlestick she'd chosen to throw at me next poised in her hand like a spear.

"Do you imagine I understand kindness when none has been given to me?" I continued. "Do you imagine it is easy to be anything other than what I am?"

"Easy? No, I do not imagine so, but change never promised to be, and if this is what you want, then you must do more than *try*."

I glared at her and then left my room, slamming the door behind me, begrudgingly returning to the prince who lived in the depths of my castle. He lay on his thin bed beneath the window, one leg hanging off and scraping the floor. The strange hat he usually wore covered his face, and his hands lay folded atop his stomach.

"Your advice did not work," I said.

The prince startled and sat up, his hat falling into his lap.

"Wh-what do you mean?"

"I told her she was beautiful, and she did not fall in love with me."

"Well, how did you say it?"

"Why does everyone keep asking that? I just...*said* it!"

"Did you mean it?"

"Yes!"

"And she didn't fall in love with you?" He seemed confused.

"I ripped the head off a selkie today. Do you really want to toy with me?"

"Of course, she must be playing hard to get," said the prince quickly. "Perhaps you should save her from danger. She will be so grateful, she will realize her love for you instantly."

"I did. Today. I saved her today."

I'd killed the selkie for what he had done to her. She had seen me holding his head and his skin.

The prince opened his mouth and then closed it. After a moment, he said, "And was she witness to your prowess?"

"Well...no."

"That's it!" he said, snapping his fingers. "You must show her your skill, your bravery. She will melt at your feet!"

"If you are wrong, I shall take the feather from your cap."

"What about my curls?" he asked.

"What curls?" I asked, a wicked smile tugging at my lips as the prince paled and smoothed his hand over his shorn hair.

117

CHAPTER TWELVE
The Bell

When I returned to my room, a metal tub full of steaming water waited. My body ached and my bones screamed, and the thought of sinking into the heat made me want to weep with relief.

I closed the door quietly and scanned the room for any signs of fae but saw none. Then I turned my attention to the water, attempting to assess if it had been enchanted. While I did, the door opened.

Naeve entered, grumbling. "What are you waiting for?" she asked. "Get in! You stink!"

I straightened. "Did you order the bath?" I asked.

"Who else?" she snapped.

"Thank you," I said.

The harsh lines carving the brownie's face softened at my gratitude, and she averted her eyes as if it made her uncomfortable.

"Hurry, hurry, before the water cools!"

I smiled at her embarrassment and reached behind

me in an attempt to loosen the laces of my dress. Casamir had tied them, and they had grown tighter over the two days I'd stayed in this gown. Naeve pushed a stool toward me, climbed it, and took over. With deft fingers, she had the dress undone in seconds. It was stiff as I pushed it down.

Once I was naked, I stepped into the bath. I could not help the moan that escaped my mouth as I sank into the water. For the first time since I'd arrived here, I felt the tension leave my body.

I could not see Naeve, but I could hear her moving about, and I knew she was near when a scrub brush popped up over the edge of the tub. It was followed shortly after by her face as she climbed the chair.

"Lean over," she said.

I hesitated and considered telling her that I could scrub my own back but decided I'd rather keep her favor, so I did as she said. When she was finished, I leaned back in the bath and immersed myself in the water, enjoying the feel of it cradling my body. When I surfaced, she scrubbed my hair until I thought my scalp might bleed before she poured a fresh bucket of water over my head without warning and then stood, holding out a towel.

My bath was finished, and as I stood and the water dripped off me, Naeve said, "Our prince is an idiot."

My brows lowered. "What?"

"Take the towel," she said and then hopped off the chair.

I stepped out of the bath, watching the brownie as she pushed the stool back to the vanity.

Once it was in place, she turned and continued, "He is an idiot, and he is not a good person. He has few positive traits, save that he is handsome, but so are all elven princes, and he will likely never understand your needs because he has never had to think of anyone but himself, but that does not mean he will not try."

"What are you talking about, Naeve?" I asked, confused by her sudden speech.

"I am trying to help you fall in love with him," she said.

"What?" I asked on a breathless laugh.

"To be sure, he has not been kind by your standards," she said, as if she had not even heard me speak. "But by the fae, he has granted you every mercy."

"What *mercy*?" I asked. "I am his prisoner, and I must *earn* my freedom, and for what? Nothing but his pleasure."

"You must earn your freedom because he cannot earn his," she said. "Trust me, it is not a pleasure to watch both of you fail at this every day."

I stared at her, confused. "What are you talking about?"

"The prince is cursed by the Glass Mountains," she said. "And if you do not guess and speak his name in five days' time, he will forget it, and if a fae does not know their name, they fade away."

"Fade away?"

"Cease to exist," she said. "Never to return to the earthly plane."

I thought of my earlier conversation with Casamir. *I have died many times and I will come back with more.* Under the curse, I supposed the cycle would cease.

"Why should I care?"

"Because now your freedom is tied to his," she said.

"And if you are not free before he forgets his name, then you never will be."

"And what does love have to do with this?" I asked.

"You can guess his name and even speak it, but you must also love him, or the curse cannot be broken."

I could not describe my shock, but the warmth that had radiated off my skin from the bath suddenly chilled me to the bone.

"Then we shall never be free," I said.

"Let us hope that is not true," she said, and with that, she left me alone to process this blow.

You must also love him.

Casamir had completely failed to communicate that part of the deal, though why would he? He needed me and likely thought himself charming enough to sway me.

"Stupid, arrogant fae prince!" I seethed aloud.

I threw off the towel and crossed to the wardrobe, knocking as I spoke.

"I need clothes! Something…*modest*!"

The door opened, and I snatched the white gown the fae offered and slipped it on as I crossed to the mirror. It was a thin night rail that did little to hide my body from sight, especially the parts of me that were still wet from the bath. I laced the ties in the front, as silly as it seemed considering that Casamir had already seen all of me. It felt like a form of rebellion.

I turned from the mirror and wandered to the window where the day was fading into night, only a small sliver of golden light peeking through the thick foliage outside.

I thought about some of the things that had occurred over the last few days—the way Casamir touched me on our first meeting, the way he'd taken over lacing my gowns, the way he had kissed me in this room as if he were starved.

But as it turned out, he was just desperate for me to fall in love with him and break a curse. My hands fisted, my face hot with shame. I crossed my arms over my chest, frustrated that I had let him indulge in my body at all.

Never again, I thought as tears pricked my eyes.

I was so embarrassed. I felt so stupid. I wasn't even sure *why*. There was nothing wrong with indulging in pleasure. Except that...I think I might have hoped that this idiot elven prince was actually *interested* in me.

"Never again," I said aloud, and I watched as the golden light turned dark red. As the light faded, I swore I heard the sound of a bell. It was a soft chime I could feel in my heart, and it drew my attention like nothing ever had before.

I pressed my ear to the window, and it became clearer—a pretty peal of bells. All at once, I felt calm, the tension and anger that had tightened my insides releasing in an instant, and I could breathe again. I drew away from the window and left, the sound growing clearer without the walls of my room in the way. I followed the portico and escaped into the garden, guided by the echoing chime.

My feet were bare and the earth was cold, but the sound of the bells was warm, so I did not mind as I made my way through towering wood lilies and shoots of anemones, between trees hung so thick with brambles and thorns, their branches were hardly visible.

The chime did not grow any louder the farther I walked, and yet I followed, as if I might find the source.

But when I came to a clearing where the ground was covered in flowering convolvuli, the sound abruptly stopped. When the bell ceased to sound, its hold on me fell away, leaving me cold and alone in the middle of the Thorn Prince's forest garden.

"Fuck," I muttered, turning in a circle at the center of the clearing, but I could no longer tell from which direction I came. Then I felt a tap on my shoulder and the color drain from my face as a familiar voice spoke.

"Do I know you?"

A knot formed in my throat, and I tried to swallow it, but I couldn't.

"Miss?"

I closed my eyes, torn between hope and horror.

I knew the voice, but I had not heard it in years.

"Darling?" Another voice joined the mix, and a sound escaped my mouth, so pained and so visceral, I could hardly hold myself up, bent beneath the anguish.

The voices were those of my dead parents.

"Darling," my mother said in her beautiful, breathy voice. It brought tears to my eyes to hear it, a long-ago echo I could never recall. "Look at my face, and you shall know that everything will be okay."

"Stop!" I said, choking on a sob that felt like a needle in my throat.

A cold hand touched my arm, and I tore away, squeezing my eyes shut tighter.

"Little one." My father's voice shook me to the core. "Listen to your mother."

"She is not my mother," I shouted, my voice raw and rough. "And you are not my father!"

"Ella."

The new voice broke me. It tore my heart out and left a gaping hole, and the blood that I saw at my feet was not my own but that of my sister.

"Do not be afraid," she said. "We are all together again."

I knew not to, but I did it anyway. I opened my eyes and beheld her. My sister, Winter. She was nothing but a corpse, a skeleton adorned in rotting flesh with an arrow lodged in her breast.

I reeled away and broke into a run, and my family followed, their shouts shrill and resonate in the wood.

"Ella! Come back!" my sister called.

"We have come to take you home," my mother said.

"Gesela! Stop running from your mother!" my father ordered in his gruff rasp.

"Go away!" I screamed and covered my ears. "Go away, go away, go away!"

I tripped, and when I hit the ground, I did not move. I felt as though my chest had been cracked open, the pain so great, I could barely breathe.

I sobbed, and my tears wet the earth beneath my head, and I only rose from where I lay when I felt something touch my cheek. I sat back and saw that it was a leaf. As I watched, the leaf sprouted a longer stem, and the stem sprouted a golden bloom, and the bloom opened to reveal a sleeping fairy. She was covered in gold. When she opened her eyes, she sat up and stretched and then smiled wickedly as she blew dust into my face.

"Fuck!" I heard Casamir curse, and the sound of his voice made my heart race in a way it never had before. I started to turn to him, but his voice cut through the air like a whip. "Close your eyes!"

His command was visceral, and I knew fairies well

enough to trust him. I did as he had ordered, and a laugh sounded from the golden fairy, small and impish, though it quickly turned into a gurgled scream.

I covered my eyes with my hands, except that they were quickly ripped away.

"No, you must look! Look!" said a voice.

I could not see the source of the power that kept me from obeying Casamir, but I was not strong enough to resist. When I opened my eyes, I saw the Prince of Thorns holding the golden fairy within his clawed hand, teeth bared as if he were about to devour her.

"Casamir!"

I did not know what possessed me to speak his name, but I did not understand anything that was happening to me anyway.

When he looked at me, I suddenly understood what the fairy had done. Her magic was desire, and as soon as Casamir's gaze connected with mine, heat erupted between my legs and an unearthly groan escaped from my mouth.

"What. Did. I. Say?" He spoke between clenched teeth. His entire body had gone rigid, and I couldn't speak, noting his heavy erection.

The fairy had gotten him too.

"Fuck," he cursed as he tossed the fairy aside. She landed with a thud and did not move as he stormed toward me and dragged me to my feet.

I thought—hoped—he would kiss me. I was ready for it, desperate for it.

My fingers tangled into his shirt as I angled my head and opened my mouth, but he turned me away and drew my back to his chest, his hands on my hips.

An unearthly whine escaped my mouth as his arousal settled against my ass. I could not help grinding into him. I arched my back and reached behind me, hoping to secure my hand behind his neck, but his hand came down on my wrist, and then he trapped my arms beneath his own.

"*Don't*," Casamir gritted out.

"Please," I begged, panting, unable to think past the desperate need pulsing throughout my entire body. I had never been this aroused.

It was more than desperation.

If he did not fuck me, I would die.

"You hate me," he said, but he pulled me closer and held me tighter. It was the smallest reprieve, the tiniest stroke of friction. I wanted to weep. "You will hate yourself."

"It's not as if we can help it," I argued.

"I'd rather not fuck someone whose lust for me is only a spell."

"Yet you had no trouble when I sucked your cock."

"That was different. *This* is different."

"How?"

"Stop talking," he said. "This is harder when you *talk*."

"Why should I?" I challenged, frustrated. "I would have never guessed the Prince of Thorns was a man of honor."

"I am not," he said, his voice grating.

He lifted and carried me beneath the branches of a nearby tree where he sat with his back to the trunk and me before him, cradled between his legs. He kept me pressed against his front, his arms trapping mine as they encircled my waist. His erection was hard between us, and despite his resistance, even he could not keep from shifting against me.

"I can ease you," I said. "I have done so before."

"*Creature,*" he warned.

"I am only asking for you. Nothing more."

He did not respond. The longer I sat there untouched, the more distressed I felt. I rubbed my thighs together to create some kind of friction, desperate to end the throbbing at the apex of my thighs.

"Please, Casamir," I begged.

"Don't. Make. This. Harder," he said between his teeth, his fingers pressing hard into my skin.

"I will die," I moaned.

His face fell into the crook of my neck, and his lips brushed over my skin as his tongue darted out to taste me. I twisted toward him, and our mouths collided in a hot and vicious kiss. I let my legs fall open, frantic for his touch, hoping he would not resist, but he kept his hands planted firmly around me. I lifted my dress and broke the kiss, letting my head fall against his shoulder as I parted my own flesh, twisting my wrist to reach deeper inside me.

"Fuck." The curse slipped from his lips.

A moan broke past my lips, and I whispered to him what I never wanted to say aloud.

"I am so wet," I said as he watched me pleasure myself over my shoulder.

"Fuck me," he whispered as his lips danced across my shoulder and up the column of my neck, teeth scraping hungrily.

"I am trying," I said, shifting my legs over his so that I was far more exposed. "Don't you want to touch me?"

"That is a foolish fucking question," he said as his teeth nibbled at my ear, but it worked.

One of his hands broke away and tangled in my hair, and he jerked my head back so he could kiss my mouth, but his action only freed me enough to pleasure myself far easier than before. As I moved inside my heat, bliss threaded throughout my body, curling deep in my belly to the point that I could no longer contain my orgasm. I opened my mouth against Casamir's as I came. When I removed my hand and reached for him, he caught it and brought my fingers to his mouth, sucking each one clean. As he did, a laugh drew our attention.

The fairy Casamir had tossed to the ground had risen, and her wicked smile returned.

"No use resisting," she said, her voice as pure as the chimes that had led me here. "It would have come to this eventually."

Casamir went rigid behind me.

"What is she talking about?" I asked.

"I do not know, but if she does not shut up, I will pluck her head from her body."

The fairy giggled again. "I only gave you what you truly wanted. Your deepest desire. It is not every day I find two people who want each other. Consider yourself lucky."

Then she fluttered away, and silence stretched between us.

"Release me," I said.

He didn't listen, his body growing tense against mine.

"Casamir," I warned, and then my hands were free. I shifted onto my knees and faced him. His eyes were dark, our need screaming between us.

128

"I hate you," I said, even as I straddled him and his hands curved against my ass.

I had to say it because what I was about to do didn't make sense.

But I wanted this.

I wanted to be wanted.

A small smile curved his lips.

"The feeling's mutual, creature."

As my mouth collided with his, Casamir tore my dress in two, each piece falling off my shoulders and pooling around my waist. I didn't care, couldn't care. My need for release had gone beyond anything rational, and I was consumed by him—by his mouth and his touch, both of which were now on my breasts.

"Is it true?" Casamir asked. "Is it true that you desire me?"

I was quiet.

"Answer the fucking question."

His hands tightened on me, his lips pressed to my neck.

"Yes," I breathed. "And you?"

The sound he made was something between a growl and a sigh.

"I knew you wanted to fuck me," he said.

"Beast," I said, pushing against him. "Answer me!"

"Yes," he growled and kissed me hard on the mouth, his hand knotted in my hair.

When he pulled away, he spoke. "You will call me Casamir if you want my cock. Do you understand?"

I parted my lips and offered a small, teasing smile. This prince was about to discover he had no control.

"Casamir," I breathed his name, my lips hovering over his.

He kissed me again, hands digging into my body as he shifted and pressed me to the ground. He sat back on his heels, eyes full of black.

"You are beautiful," he said, and this time when he spoke, I knew he meant it.

Then he shed his clothes, and his cock was thick and full. He settled between my hips, only wearing the silver chains, which were cold as they rested against my skin. I sighed with relief at the feel of him against me, widening my legs so that his crown rested within my heat.

He paused for a moment and brushed my hair from my face. The movement was strangely gentle, and then he spoke, voice warm and low. "I will give you everything," he said. "But right now—"

"You have never been charming," I said, interrupting him. "Do not waste my time with it now."

He smiled shrewdly and then pushed inside me in one fluid movement. I hadn't known how much I needed this until now. We both groaned, and I let my head fall back against the ground as his fingers wrapped around the column of my neck, though he did not press. As much as I hated to surrender to this creature, lying beneath him right now, it only seemed right.

"Choke me," I said.

He did not need encouragement, and I had expected this because since our first encounter, he had had an obsession with my neck. As he gently squeezed and thrust inside me, I thought I might die from the rush of pleasure that blossomed throughout my body, only growing in intensity as he continued to press on either side of my neck.

I grasped his forearm and tried to take a breath

when my chest started to burn. He loomed over me, watching my face, and then he bent to kiss my mouth before releasing me. I took a deep, guttural breath, light-headed but so fucking aroused I could barely hold on to my orgasm. I did not want this to end because beneath Casamir's heated gaze, I felt like *someone*.

"So fucking beautiful, so fucking wet," he said, panting, but he whispered the words, as if he were only speaking to himself. Then his hand returned to my neck and his pace shifted into something far more visceral and carnal. I loved it and wanted it more than I had ever wanted anything, even my freedom.

When he released me, I came, but he continued to move, chasing his own release.

"Come inside me," I said.

"Fuck you," he breathed, but he planted his arms on either side of my head and leaned close, and I reveled in the crush of his body against mine. Perspiration gathered on his brow, and I held on to him, fingers pressing into his skin until he kissed me, coming with his mouth against mine.

I wrapped my legs around him to keep him inside me, expecting him to soften, expecting to find myself sated, but as the prince pulled back and met my gaze, the fire that had spurred us on from the start reignited.

"What kind of magic is this?" I moaned as I arched against him.

"This is not magic," he said and bent to press a kiss to my neck, then my jaw. It was a sweet gesture, and it sent a strange feeling of comfort throughout my body, even as the heat from our coupling raged inside me. "This is *need*."

If this was need, I had never known it before, but I was certain I could not live without it, and I had sense enough to feel the dread of that thought before I was consumed once more by passion for the elven prince whose name I did not know.

CHAPTER THIRTEEN
Enchantment

I was only half-awake, but there was a part of me that was aware of the heat and hardness pressed against my back and how heavy Casamir's arms were around me. The longer I lay there, the more I became aware of my body and the places where I ached. Despite how exhausted I felt, a fire still raged beneath my skin, desperate to take this elven prince inside me once again.

I had to be enchanted, I told myself, but even I knew that was not true. If either of us were still under the fairy's spell, we would not have fallen asleep. We would have continued to come together beneath this cursed sky.

What was wrong with me?

Casamir was my jailor. He was a beast.

He was fae and he lived within a place that had taken so much from me.

I could not do this. I could not let this happen again no matter how much I wanted him.

Desperately.

Casamir stirred, and as he moved, I sat up, my back to him. It seemed wrong to face him, especially in the aftermath of what we had done, though I wanted to. We were not lovers, and I had no tender feelings toward him.

I couldn't, though that thought made my chest ache.

I felt his eyes on me, and after a moment, he spoke.

"Are you well?"

The question straightened my spine.

It was the last thing I expected him to say. I thought he would taunt me, remind me of how he had known I wanted him.

I swallowed and turned my head to the side to answer. I still could not look at him.

"I...don't know."

"Did I hurt you?"

"No," I answered quickly. "No, you didn't."

We were silent after that, and I remained where I was, even as Casamir stood. I was not certain what he was doing, but after a moment, he walked into view, half-dressed, his tunic in hand. My eyes trailed up his front, and I met his dark gaze.

"Will you come with me?" he asked.

Perhaps it was because he had asked and not commanded, but I placed my hand in his without question, and when his fingers closed around mine, warmth blossomed throughout my body at the thought of everything these hands had done to me.

He helped me to my feet and trailed a finger across my cheek and then over a spot on my shoulder, frowning.

"You lied," he said.

I lowered my brows. "What do you mean?"

But when I looked at the place he traced on my skin, I saw what he meant. I was scratched and bruised.

But so was he.

I met his gaze.

"It's…not as if you could help it," I said.

Still he frowned, but his fingers tightened, and he tugged me along through a curtain of trees and down a sloping hill. At the bottom was a small body of water that was fed by a trickling waterfall. Here, I could see nothing beyond the thick wood.

Casamir dropped his tunic to the mossy ground, and the rest of his clothes followed.

"I thought you might want to bathe," he said.

I stared at him for a few seconds before my gaze shifted to the shimmering pool. It was beautiful and felt isolated, though I did not trust it was private.

"It's safe," Casamir said, and when I met his gaze, he added, "I promise."

From a fae, those words bore the weight of a blood oath. Despite what he had promised, I could not help thinking about how the selkie had attacked me, and though he was dead, the memories had me hesitating at the edge of the water.

I felt Casamir approach, and he touched my side with the tips of his nails.

"Do you trust me?" he asked, his mouth close to my ear.

I took a breath, turning toward him slightly.

"This second, yes, but I can promise nothing beyond this moment."

He pressed a kiss to my shoulder, and his hand flattened against the small of my back as he guided me into the lake. I stood for a few moments in the water, thigh-deep, and when nothing happened, I dove beneath the water to put distance between us. When I broke the surface, I faced him.

He had not moved, and I could not place the expression on his face. It was dark and sensual. It made me feel desired and it also scared me.

"Why did you leave the palace?" he asked.

"I heard a bell," I said, and even now as I thought about the sound, the beauty of it brought tears to my eyes. "And I could not help but follow."

"Where did it lead?"

"To my dead family," I said.

His jaw tightened and I expected him to ask about them, but he didn't.

"The bell was the mountains' hold over you," he said. "Your family...that was the fairies."

I did not ask why because I knew. Casamir had warned me about the mountains, and the selkie had warned me about the fairies and their retribution.

"Naeve tells me you are cursed," I said.

Casamir did not react.

"What did you do?"

He waded farther into the lake, and I tracked him as he moved, but he did not speak until he dipped below the water and resurfaced, his dark hair plastered to his face.

"I slept with a daughter of the Mountains," he said. "And she fell hopelessly in love with me, and because I did not return her love, the Mountains cursed me to forget my true name."

"Unless it's spoken with love," I said. "Isn't that right?"

He only stared at me.

"Is that what you hoped for from me?"

The hollows of his cheeks deepened as he ground his teeth.

"I do not hope for anything," he said.

We circled one another.

"I cannot believe that no one has fallen in love with you."

"Many have," he said. "But none are clever enough to guess my name."

"And if I do not guess, you will cease to exist?"

"Eventually," he said, and then he smiled, reaching to draw a piece of my hair behind my ear. "Something for you to look forward to."

I wanted to argue, to tell him I would never feel that way, but the words were stuck in my throat, and I swallowed hard.

We did not speak after that, and once we had finished swimming in the lake, we came to shore.

"Put this on," Casamir said, offering his tunic. It was a reminder of how I had come here and how I was leaving, my nightdress torn in two, a mark of the desperation we had felt to be inside each other.

A rush of warmth burned my skin.

I took his tunic and slipped it over my head. There was an element of regret as his smell surrounded me, and it pulled at memories from long ago when I would climb to the roof of my parent's cottage with my sister and watch as the sun rose, the morning light catching on the dewdrops, making our little hollow glimmer.

I used to think it was magic, but now I knew otherwise.

Magic was the darkness that existed between the trees, the place where light did not shine, and it had taken everything.

"Are you so regretful?"

I opened my eyes and looked up at Casamir, whose features were harsh but not angry. I could not tell exactly how he felt, but there was a tightness to his mouth and eyes that made me think that he was struggling, but with what, I did not know.

"It is not as if we can help what happened," I said and looked away before I could see his reaction. I was too afraid to know what he was thinking or how he really felt. What if he regretted me?

"Will you not look at me?" he asked.

So I did. We glared at one another, a tension building between us that I could not exactly place, but it was hurt and angry and strange, and even with all those emotions, I still felt a keen desire for him.

"How much do you hate me now?" he asked.

I ground my teeth and lowered my brows. All I could manage to say was, "I don't hate you...not for this."

I did not think that would make him angrier, and yet his eyes darkened and his jaw ticked, and this time, he looked away.

"Come."

We left and I remained a step behind him as he led me from the clearing in the woods where our madness had come to a head. He was shirtless and the muscles in his shoulders rippled with each tiny movement. His back was scored with red lines from my fingernails. I liked that I had marked him in some way, but the fact that others would see it and *know* embarrassed me, though I wasn't sure why I cared.

Perhaps it was because I was supposed to hate him.

I was supposed to hate him and…I didn't.

Why don't I hate him?

It was not as if he'd done anything to deserve my favor, but there had been a few strange and tender moments last night that had made me feel something beyond the cold anger that had seethed inside me for years. For once, I had not been invisible or forgotten or alone.

Casamir paused and held out his hand to halt me. The sudden stop made my heart race, and I looked at him as he spoke.

"Stay here," he said. "I'll only be gone a moment."

Anything could happen in a moment within his woods, but I stayed where I'd stopped and did not move a single muscle as he vanished into the surrounding trees, returning a moment later as he had said with a red apple in hand.

"Here," he said, holding it out to me. "It's safe to eat. I promise."

Promise.

I liked that word coming from his lips, and I wanted to hear it more. I should have said so, but the strain between us had only grown since we had begun our journey back, so I held on to those words.

I took the apple but only stared at him.

"What's this for?"

He shrugged and looked a little uncomfortable. "I thought…you might be hungry."

I laughed. I couldn't help it. His actions were so contrary to what I had expected. But he remained very serious, so I pressed my lips together to keep quiet and then cleared my throat.

"Thank you," I said, and I took a bite from the apple, which was crisp and sweet, noting that Casamir watched my mouth as I ate.

He seemed to realize he was staring and then turned away.

"We should get back."

We did not speak for the rest of the walk, and when the castle came into view, I felt a sense of dread. I did not know where it came from or what spurred it until Casamir paused and faced me. Suddenly, I realized I did not know how to move beyond this point. There was no going back to whatever had existed between us before, and while that had not been easy, it was better than this strange longing inside me now.

"I," he began but did not continue.

"What?" I prompted.

He took a moment to speak, but as he did, his tone became more biting.

"Another letter from my true name." I could not help feeling disgusted by his words, and still he continued. "Did you not set the rules for our encounters? A letter for each time I come by your hand?"

I was so shocked by his words, I couldn't think, could do nothing but strike him. My hand stung, and his cheek was red.

"How dare you."

He did not flinch, did not even press his hand to the mark on his face to soothe the pain.

"I only thought I should give you something you wouldn't regret."

"When it comes to you, Casamir, I regret *everything*."

I turned from him and fled.

The sooner I learned his true name, the better.

I had to get out of here.

CHAPTER FOURTEEN

Rule of Three

I watched my creature retreat with all the fury of a storm.
I did not understand her. Perhaps I did not want to. I
had given her what she wanted, offered her a letter from
my name so that her shame might not feel so heavy, and
instead of expressing gratitude, she had struck me.

It is because you are an idiot.

The mirror's voice echoed in my mind, and I ground
my teeth against his words.

"She clearly regretted our time together," I said
aloud.

Did you ask her what she regrets?

"She said it!"

*Only after you offered a letter. Perhaps she was not so
regretful but more embarrassed.*

"They are the same."

They are not the same.

"You expect me to rejoice that my creature was
embarrassed about our time together?"

Perhaps it has nothing to do with you, said the mirror, who paused and then added, *Idiot*.

I pressed my hand to my face, but the memory of her lived beneath my skin and all over my body. I knew I would never be rid of this hold she had on me. It was just as strong as the Mountains that had cursed me, and I did not know why, but I felt it with more certainty than I had anything else in my long life. It felt silly to think such a thing, especially in the aftermath of what we had done, but I had had sex with many, many people, and I had never felt this way before.

Perhaps this was the Mountains' attempt to curse me further. Had they taken her flesh only to make me crave it?

You have always craved it. You have always craved her. You only expected that your appetite would ebb once you had a taste, but it has only made you ravenous.

I left the garden outside my palace and went to visit the mortal prince, who was standing on the bench beneath his window, hands wrapped around the bars.

"I will give you anything you desire if you tell my father where I am being held prisoner," he was saying.

"Careful of offering desires," I said. "That is a good way to end up giving away your firstborn."

The prince froze and turned toward me, his eyes wide with fear.

"Don't...don't kill me."

"I will not kill you," I said. "But I will settle for stripping you of what you hold most dear."

"You mean my hair and the red feather in my hat?"

"I have not yet taken the feather in your hat," I said. "But I will take it now."

The mortal was wearing his hat over his shorn hair, and the feather vanished from it with a pop. He did not take it off to check that it was gone.

"So you saved her from danger, and she still does not love you?"

I knew she did not love me, but there were moments when she looked at me differently since last night, and I did not know what they meant or if they were even real.

"When you rescued your princess, what happened?"

The prince shrugged. "She was grateful."

"And?"

"And?" he repeated, confused.

"What else happened?"

"We returned to her kingdom where her father declared that we would wed," he said. Then he asked, "Did you rescue your princess?"

"I did," I said.

"And what happened?"

"I fucked her in the woods all night long."

The prince gasped and his eyes widened. "You... Are you married?"

"Do I *look* married?"

"Well, not exactly, but you cannot...*fuck*...a lady until you have married her. You will ruin her!"

I raised a brow. "Have you never had sex?"

"Not with a lady. I am *honorable*."

The prince might be many things, but honorable certainly wasn't one.

I frowned. "How is sex not honorable?"

The prince hesitated. "I...I don't know."

"Then why do you speak on things you do not know?"

The mortal was quiet and then he asked, "Do you love this woman? The one you fucked in the woods?"

I did not know what to say.

"You must," said the prince more to himself than to me. "Or you would not want her to love you."

"Do not presume to know how I feel, mortal," I hissed. "I *need* her to love me."

I needed her to speak my true name.

"At some point, if you do not love her, someone else will."

"What do you know about love?" I countered. "All your advice has only made my creature hate me more."

"What worked for my princess may not work for yours. Have you tried asking her what she wants?"

She wanted freedom, and that was beyond what I could give even if I wanted to. Magic was binding. She was the only person who could free herself now, and her choices were to speak my name or live out the next six years while I descended into madness and eventually ceased to exist.

"What if she does not tell me?"

"Then I suppose you will take something else from me."

CHAPTER FIFTEEN
A Riddle

The prince of thorns is an idiot, *I thought as I* sprawled on my bed, staring up at the bland ceiling.

I wanted to hate him.

I was definitely angry with him, especially at how we had parted this morning. After everything we had shared, he'd thought to diminish it by offering a letter from his true name.

An *I*.

I already had a *U*.

I should feel excited. It was two steps closer to guessing Casamir's true name, and all I needed were five more letters, but I could only think of last night. It wasn't even the most passionate parts that clung to my memories now. It was the moments when the cruel elven prince had gently kissed my forehead and asked if I was okay, when he had offered his shirt and then the apple, when he had expressed concern over my wellness and feared he had hurt me.

He had made me *feel* things...not just desire but *desired*.

He had done all that and then ruined it with a stupid letter.

Why is he an idiot? I fumed.

I tried not to think about him but failed.

I had already softened toward him, had already felt the long-forgotten rise of hope inside me, and now that it was awakened, I could do nothing but wallow in misery and try to convince myself that nothing that had happened last night was real.

Except that every time I looked in the mirror, I saw reminders of his touch—bruises and swollen skin—and I could recall every action that had led to each blemish.

Those thoughts drove me from my room and motivated me to search the castle for any clues that might lead to Casamir's true name—if they existed. I only hoped I could avoid the elven prince as I roamed his corridors, but as I did, I noted how this place was far from personal.

If I had wandered here on my own, I would have assumed the castle was abandoned with its moss-covered walls and flowering vines crawling from floor to ceiling. There were no portraits, not even of himself, and instead of soft carpet, there was an array of ground cover—vines, shrubs, mosses—at my feet. One fed into the other as I turned down each winding hall, pausing to look out windows that were either draped with vines or obscured with thick branches from trees that had grown into the facade of the castle.

There was no doubt about its beauty, though I wondered if all elves lived this way.

I came to the end of a hall where a set of stairs rose into darkness. I looked about before I took them, slow and steady as they wound upward and opened into a large bedchamber. While the colors in the room were dark and grounding, there were four floor-to-ceiling windows that made the room bright and full of light.

A large four-poster bed sat against one wall, each post richly carved, and the curtains that hung to veil the bed were open and dark green in color. A broken mirror hung between two of the large windows.

I realized I had been here before, that this was where Casamir's five brothers had sent me at the start of my punishment. I remembered the soft carpet at my feet and the hearth and fireplace nearby.

Unlike the other rooms, the plant life was contained to a corner where several shelves were lined with flowers, vines, and weeping greenery. It was strange, considering the whole castle was overgrown in flora.

"You must be the mortal our prince is obsessed with."

I gasped and turned to see who was speaking, but no one was there.

"Who's there?" I asked.

"Over here," said the voice, which sounded like it came from the windows.

I crossed to look behind the heavy curtains.

"No, no. The mirror," said the voice.

My brows lowered as I stepped in front of the broken shard of glass, but I saw nothing, not even my reflection. I started to peek behind it, thinking that perhaps a fae was playing a trick.

"What are you doing?"

I gasped and released the mirror. It clanked lightly against the wall.

"I thought you might be fae," I said.

"I told you I was a mirror."

"Have you always been a mirror?"

"Yes. What kind of question is that?"

"I thought you might have been cursed."

"I am not cursed. I am enchanted."

"What is the difference?"

"Perspective, I suppose."

I stood, silent for a moment, before the mirror.

"You are the Magic Mirror," I said, recalling my conversation with Wolf about how Casamir's father had deemed the next king would be chosen.

"So you have heard of me," he said, his voice filling with pride.

"I do not know much, I am afraid. Only that you are not whole."

"There is not much to know beyond that," he said.

I turned to look around the room. "So this must be Casamir's chamber?"

Though I had been here before, I had not taken the time to observe. I had been too consumed by the elven lord in front of me to focus on anything other than him and survival.

"Have you come in search of him?" he said.

"No," I said. "I would rather not see him today or tomorrow, perhaps not ever again."

"That does not bode well for him," said the mirror.

I glanced at the mirror. "You know about the curse?"

"*You* know about the curse?" he asked.

I stared at the mirror, and I think he stared back. We were both silent.

"If you have not come for Casamir, then why are you here?"

"I came in search of his true name," I said.

"Ah," said the mirror. "You will not find answers here."

"Where will I find them?"

I imagined that the mirror shrugged as he answered, "Here and there."

I ground my teeth, frustrated. I walked to the end of Casamir's bed, and all I could think, all I could imagine, was us, tangled together in a sea of dark silk. If we had sex again, would it be different? Would he be gentler, sweeter, far more protective?

It all made me too angry. I should not even be thinking about a next time. I should be focused on my goal of getting out of here.

I ground my teeth and turned to look at the mirror, leaning against the end of Casamir's bed.

"Do you always watch him?" I asked.

"I have no choice," he said. "I am a mirror."

"Does he…" I started. "Does he have…visitors?"

"He does not," said the mirror.

I hated the relief that unfurled in my body, hated that I had asked at all.

"Why does he keep these plants when his whole castle is a garden?" I asked.

"He loves them," said the mirror. "That is why the castle is a garden."

My brows lowered and I crossed again to the corner where all his plants were on display. Suddenly I saw his home in a new light. I had thought there was nothing personal about it, but the whole thing…it was a reflection of what he loved.

Something warm filled my chest.

"Why does he love plants?"

"I imagine it is because with plants, he can be who he truly is without consequence."

"And who is Casamir?" I asked. "Truly?"

"I think you know," said the mirror. "The question is, are you willing to see it?"

I pursed my lips and crossed my arms, feeling strangely exposed.

"Where is he?"

"I can show you," said the mirror. "Though you may not wish to know."

I waited and watched as the mirror's surface warped and changed, and I saw Casamir waist-deep in water. He was washing a spray of blood and gold dust from his body. I did not think I needed to know what he had killed. I could guess. The fae who had drawn me into their trap last night, the fae who had blown into my face and made me ache for him.

His features were hard, and there was a part of me that wanted to trace away the tension between his brows and his mouth. I followed his hands, trailing over the hard muscles of his shoulders and arms, his chest and stomach, before he disappeared below the surface of the lake.

When he rose again, he waded to the shore. As his body was slowly revealed to me, I could not help but ache for him again, and as much as I wanted this to be magic, I knew it wasn't.

I took a deep breath and turned from the mirror.

"How do I find his true name?"

I had to find it. I had to speak it.

"You don't," he said. "It will find you."

"How? How when no one knows it?"

"Everyone knows his name. It knows no stranger. It is the wail on the lips of a birthing mother, the howl from the mouth of a grieving lover. It is the cry that breaks the night when death is summoned and the scream that echoes at daybreak when truth makes you ache."

"I am not looking to solve a riddle," I said, frustrated by his words but also processing them, feeling them. "I need a name."

"You know his name," said the mirror. "You have felt it."

I considered what he had said and could acknowledge that I knew what it was to watch death arrive and steal away life. I knew what it was to wish through the night that it wasn't true. I knew what it was to have my heart broken each morning at daybreak.

"I know grief, that is true," I said. "But grief is not a name."

"Anything can be a name," said the mirror. "But you are right. Grief is not Casamir's true name."

We were silent for a moment, and then the mirror said, "Think on it, creature. You have four days."

CHAPTER SIXTEEN
Love Me, Leave Me

I waited for my creature to come as I had called, just outside the entrance to the dining room dressed in my finest robes. I felt ridiculous and uncomfortable and the anticipation was driving me mad. It ate within my chest like a seething parasite. Why did I feel this way? I had seen her before, a hundred times, but this time was different because I had been inside her. I had given her pleasure and she had writhed beneath me, and I wanted that again even if she did not.

I was not prepared for her when she came into view. She had always been beautiful, but tonight she was exquisite. She wore a fitted gown, as thin as fairy wings. The colors changed as she moved, from pink to gold.

The elves in her wardrobe had done well, the best since she had arrived.

She stopped in front of me, and we stared at each other in a strange and uncomfortable silence.

"You look beautiful," I said, and I hoped she could tell how much I meant it.

Her chest rose as she took a deep breath. "Thank you."

I held out my hand for her. It took her a moment to accept, and when she did, I pulled her to me. Her eyes widened, and one of her hands pressed flat against my chest but she did not push me away.

I held her gaze and brushed a finger along her cheek.

"I want you," I said, and the truth of it echoed in my bones.

"A letter," she said, her voice quiet and her eyes lowered to my lips. "And you can have me."

Anger twisted through me like a knife.

I wanted her to want me too. I wanted her to want me without expectation, though there was a part of me that knew I had done this when I had given her a letter this morning.

"A letter," I said. "And you will serve me dinner. Naked."

She pushed away from me.

"Fuck you."

"I'd really rather not talk about fucking," I said, scowling.

The mood between us changed rapidly, and a thick tension descended. I hated the feel of it, making me feel overdressed and on edge.

"You are despicable," she said.

"Then be free of me sooner and accept the fucking offer."

"I thought you didn't want to talk about fucking," she spat.

We glared at each other, and then she lifted her head, chin jutting out, eyes flashing confidently. "Two letters."

"Fine," I said and turned from her, stalking into the dining room where I took a seat at the head of the table.

"Undress," I ordered.

"The letters," she said.

"A," I said. "The other after you are naked."

"I hate you," she said.

"The feeling is mutual, mortal."

"Fu—"

I stood, the chair scraping against the floor as I did, silencing her. My hand came down flat on the table, the sound echoing in the dining room.

"What did I say?"

She glared, her eyes gleaming, and with her silence, I sat. She reached behind her and managed to loosen the ties of her dress. I would have liked to help, would have liked to feel her skin against my fingertips as her dress pooled to the floor, but I knew she did not want that. Still, it was a pleasure to watch her. She was glorious. I shifted uncomfortably, my arousal growing long and hard.

"Why are you angry?" she asked.

"You make me angry. You make me insane," I said.

"You asked for this."

"*You* asked for this!" I said. "Words in this world are binding, vicious creature, or have you learned nothing living in its shadow?"

Her fists clenched.

"Give me the second letter, bastard."

"S," I said. "Are you pleased?"

"I will never be pleased by you."

"We both know differently, creature."

"That was *not* a choice."

"But it was a desire, was it not? No matter how much you wish it wasn't."

She was silent as she crossed to the table where the food had been piled among glittering candles, choosing to ladle soup from a silver tureen.

As she worked, she glanced at me.

"What happened to your nails?"

I fisted my hand so she could not see them, though it was too late.

"I cut them," I said. Because they had hurt her, because I could not pleasure her with claws.

The choice seemed silly now in the face of her hate.

She said nothing, and once the bowl was full, she crossed to me, spit in it, and placed it on the table in front of me.

I could feel her eyes on me as I stared at it, quiet and still, before swiping it off the table and reaching for my creature's wrist. I stood and pulled her to me, trapping her against the table. As I settled my hips against hers, she gasped. I twined my fingers into her hair and pulled her head back.

"Not a choice?" I whispered as I trailed my lips over her taut neck. "Are you certain, creature?"

Her hands tightened in my shirt.

I reached for the closest bottle of wine, uncorked it, took a drink, and kissed her with the liquid in my mouth, feeding it to her as I tasted her. It spilled from our mouths as our lips and tongues moved desperately together.

She did not push me away, so I guided her onto the

edge of the table, and when her thighs parted around me, I pulled away.

"Do you want this?" I asked.

"What is this?" she asked.

I smirked and spoke, my lips hovering over hers. "My mouth. My tongue. My fingers. *Me*."

She stared at me, and when she did not answer, I began to pull away, but her hands fisted in my shirt, halting me.

"No," she said.

"No?" I asked.

"I mean yes," she said, breathless. "Yes. I want this."

I had never felt such relief, and I kissed her for it before pulling back again to look at her.

"Fucking beautiful," I said, appreciating how she was spread before me, legs parted, her breasts heavy, her eyes hooded. "I will show you what it would be like if you were to stay with me forever. The pleasure I will give you. The care I will take. You will beg for it. You will love it."

You will love me, I thought. I hoped.

I took the wine, and she gasped as I poured it over her body. Trails of deep red beaded down her skin, over her breasts and down her stomach, pooling in her navel and over the dark curls between her thighs. When I was finished, I bent and licked the bittersweet liquid from her. I started with her pillowy breasts, taking each into my mouth and sucking her nipples into harder peaks. Her back arched, her body curving toward mine, and her fingers glided through my hair, nails scraping my scalp.

I moved down her stomach, kissing and letting my tongue swirl and taste, sucking parts of her skin into my mouth until her breath caught. I had no motive save her pleasure, knowing she had chosen this without the influence of a fairy.

Tomorrow, she could not run from this.

I came to her hips and kissed each before letting my lips feather across her thighs. Her breaths were short and shallow, and she squirmed beneath me. I let my tongue touch her heat and she groaned, offering a keen whimper as I pulled away. I met her gaze as she reached for me, guiding my head between her legs.

"Touch me. Casamir, *please.*"

"Remember that you begged," I said, and then I let myself have her. I licked her slowly. I licked every fold. She tasted so good, she tasted so sweet, and I buried my face in her, chasing her as she wiggled beneath me. I moved to her clit, which was swollen and full, heated against my tongue. I licked it and sucked it, and as I touched her there, I let my fingers slide inside her.

She gave a guttural cry and lifted off the table. I pressed my hand down on her stomach to keep her in place, looking up from my place between her thighs, watching as her head rolled back against the table, her hands squeezing her breasts.

Fuck me. She was glorious.

My lust was so acute, my cock hard to the point of aching. I wanted to be inside her again, I wanted to feel her come around me, but I would settle for this tonight. If she wanted more, she would have to come to me.

My creature's heels dug into my shoulders, her knees fell open, and she moved against my mouth, grinding harder, writhing. When she came, it was decadent and delicious, and I kept my mouth against her until she went slack. Then I climbed up her body and kissed her, my tongue stroking hers until I could no longer taste her.

Her hands tangled in my hair and dug into my scalp. Her legs wrapped around my waist, sealing our bodies together, and then she tore her mouth from mine.

"I need you inside me," she said.

"Do you need me?" I asked, breathless. "Or do you want me?"

"Does it matter?" she asked. "I have asked. I have begged."

"Want or need, vicious thing?"

She pushed against my chest, and I straightened, staring down at her as she sat there, marked and rosy by my mouth.

"Do you not want me?" she asked.

"That is a foolish question," I said.

I was desperate for her.

Her eyes lowered to my erection, which strained against the fabric of my trousers, and darkened. Her foot caressed me there, teasing.

"Then take me," she said. "I am offering."

"You will regret it," I said. "As you regretted last night."

Her eyes hardened, and as much as I hated to deny her, I did not trust that she wanted me. She was caught in a haze of pleasure, and in this state, she would welcome me even if she did not truly want me, and that would bring her no closer to loving me.

She pushed off the table and leaned forward on the tips of her toes, her face close to mine.

"Coward," she said, letting the word slip between her teeth.

Then she snatched her dress from the floor and fled.

CHAPTER SEVENTEEN
Sweet Poison

I raced to my room, stumbling, blinded by tears I refused to shed for that…*pathetic* excuse of a *man* who was not a man at all but a horrible, conniving, vicious elf. When I was safely in my room, I leaned against the door and closed my eyes, waiting until my heart rate eased, until the heat in my face lessened, until I had swallowed enough that the tears no longer threatened to release.

What did he *want* from me?

I had done everything he had asked.

He said "Beg," so I begged.

I should rejoice that he had stopped, because what had I been thinking? I had been so caught up in the pleasure of his mouth, his touch, I was willing to compromise myself further, and this time I would not have an excuse for enjoying him because I had been under no enchantment.

But instead, I only felt ashamed, ridiculous, rejected, because in the end…I had truly wanted him.

How could I want him?

He was an elven prince, and I was his captive.

I pushed away from the door and threw the gown I had worn to dinner into the corner of the room. I wasn't even sure why I had bothered to dress. I should have worn the sheer robe the elves in the wardrobe had crafted. It would have been more fitting for what Casamir had planned.

That thought made me angrier.

He had humiliated me, and in exchange for what? A few letters—*U*, *I*, *A*, *S*—four of seven that were completely useless.

The more I thought about it, the angrier I grew. I snatched my robe off the end of my bed and slipped it on as I reached for my ax. The handle was still full of thorns, but I did not care that they pricked my hand as I ventured out of my room and made my way to Casamir's bedroom in the dark.

I held my ax aloft, the stab of each thorn in my hand sharp, my hand already sticky with blood. I was unsure of what might come my way in the night, but I was so full of rage, I was willing to fight just about anything. Perhaps the fae knew not to tempt me, because I made it to Casamir's room with no trouble.

Despite how determined I was, I hesitated, standing outside his door. I felt a deep sense of dread...a knowledge that once I entered here, I would not come out, and yet I wished to end this. To end him.

I touched the handle of his door and turned it carefully. I slipped into his room and approached his bedside, parting the curtains slightly to look at him. A slice of moonlight cut across his bare chest.

"Have you come to kill me?" he asked.

I did not answer but climbed onto his bed. It was tall and I felt clumsy as I struggled to keep hold of my ax, each sharp point digging farther into my skin. He did not move as I straddled him, just looked at me with those gleaming eyes.

I held my ax close to my chest. He did not try to take it, but he did frown as he observed the blood seeping between my fingers.

"You are wounded."

I lifted my weapon over my head and held it there. I wanted to hurt him, but I also wanted to fuck him.

"If you are going to do it, aim for my head," he said.

"Which one?" I asked. "The one I am looking at or the one between my thighs?"

"If you cut off the one between your thighs, you likely will not get what you came for."

I lowered the ax a little. "I want to hate you."

"I know," he said, his voice quiet, and as he rose to me, he wrapped his hand around my wrist and his mouth collided with mine.

I lowered the ax, letting it fall to the floor. He gripped my face, fingers digging into my scalp. I held on to his forearms, unsure what I intended, only knowing that now I could not think beyond the pleasure of his mouth moving against mine, demanding my complete submission. I was ready for it. I opened to it, and when his tongue moved past my lips to coil with mine, I sighed into his mouth and my body relaxed into his. My arms slipped around his neck, and I crushed myself to him, relishing the feel of his arousal against me as I shifted closer, addicted to the way he made me feel—completely lost and not of this world.

Casamir broke away and his hands tightened in my hair. As he pulled my head back, he growled against my throat.

"You are poison, sweet creature. I want you in my blood."

Then he sucked my skin into his mouth until a cry broke from my lips, and once it had, he pushed me onto my back and sat on his heels, staring down at me.

"Thank fuck for wicked fairies," he said as his eyes skimmed over my body, veiled by the sheer robe. The longer he looked and did not touch, the more impatient I became, warmed and writhing.

I reached for the tie at my waist, but Casamir stopped me.

"Let me," he said.

I held his gaze. "You have seen me like this before."

"And it will never be enough."

I stared, unable to fully comprehend his tone, but he spoke as if he were reciting an oath, sincere but forlorn, and it shifted something inside me.

I let my hands fall away and gripped the blankets beneath me as he pulled the tie and parted my robe. And though it hid nothing, he acted as if he had unveiled the most precious gems in the world.

He bent and pressed a kiss to my stomach, his eyes meeting mine for only a moment, burning like coals in the darkness.

Then he kissed me again and again, trailing down to my thighs. I fisted the blankets and arched my back. I would have rubbed my thighs together just for the sake of friction, but Casamir was between them, teasing me with featherlight kisses.

He smiled at my desperate writhing.

"Casamir," I said, my chest so tight with anticipation, I could barely take in air.

"Yes, sweet creature?"

His voice rumbled against my skin.

"This is torture."

"Ah," he said, lips grazing the bottom of my stomach. "But is it good?"

"It could be better," I said.

"Is that so?" he whispered. "How?"

"Touch me."

"I am touching you."

I gave a guttural cry and reached for his head, but he pushed me flat against the bed with one hand and used the other to spread me apart. But all he did was stare.

"Forgive me, sweet creature," he said. "You must be starved."

Then he licked me, circling my clit, and I thought I might die from the rush of it, from the sheer pleasure that twisted low in my stomach and threaded throughout my body.

"Fuck." I lowered toward him, spreading my legs farther, and he took the invitation, slipping a finger inside me, then two. "Yes."

It did not matter that he had just done this earlier; it felt even better now. His touch and tongue were different, far more intense. I felt all of him and everything, as if my body were one exposed nerve, every part of me pulsating around him.

I never expected this strange fae to become the center of my universe, but I would lie beneath him forever if I could feel like this every second of every day.

Here, where there was no pain and no loss.

Here, where I was not alone.

I reached for his head, grinding into him, and a sound I had never made came from deep in my throat as he chased my pleasure. The pressure built and built, and I could no longer contain the sounds escaping my mouth.

"Yes, yes, yes," I whispered until my words broke on a sob, and I came against his mouth so hard my body shook. As Casamir pulled away and pressed kisses to my lower stomach and up and over my chest, he was breathless, and still, he kissed me, desperate, as if he had gone too long without me.

His body was warm and damp against mine. I reached between us and wrapped my fingers around his cock. He was hard and soft at the same time, and he groaned against my mouth as I touched him.

When he pulled away, he must have understood the desire in my eyes because he drew his finger over my lips and answered, "Only if you wish it."

I would correct him and tell him I never wish for anything, but this, I wished for.

We traded positions, and as he stretched before me, I stared, eyes roving the planes of his chest and the swell of his arousal, which pressed against his stomach. He was beautiful and it made my heart ache.

I met his gaze.

"You were made for this," I said.

He smiled and asked, "Made for what, sweet creature?"

Pleasure, I wanted to say. *Sex*.

But instead, I answered, "Heartbreak."

He remained still, but there was an edge to his expression that told me he did not disagree. If he was going to speak, I did not know, because I kissed him, pressing my lips to his stomach as he had done to mine.

He held himself up but reclined, moving my hair over my shoulder. I could feel his cock between my breasts as I moved down his body, and when the crown touched my chin, I shifted and closed my mouth over the tip.

Casamir took a breath, and I looked up at him as I released him and licked him from root to tip before taking him into my mouth again. He braced his hands behind him, his head falling back, neck exposed as I worked.

His breath came heavier and he moaned louder. His fingers threaded through my hair, but they did not tighten.

"Fuck," he said, his voice airy. "You are a sweet thing."

Come beaded thickly from the tip of his cock, and it tasted salty on my tongue. I thought of all the times he had come inside me last night, how I had demanded it and wanted it again.

I did not know what he was feeling as I touched him and sucked him, but I felt the power of having him in my hands and mouth—I controlled his very breath, and right now it was ragged.

It made me ache for him, and when I released him, I climbed up his body and pressed my mouth hard to his before rolling so that I was beneath him.

He rested between my legs, fingers brushing strands of my hair from my face.

"Are you sure about this?" he asked, studying my face, searching for something beyond the confirmation I spoke.

He wanted to know that I would not have regret.

"I came," I said. "And you did not have to call."

He stared, then his eyes dropped to my lips, and he kissed me softly and lushly, letting his hips press into me before he rose onto all fours. As he shifted closer, I widened and lifted my hips. He drew the head of his cock along my entrance and slid inside.

I took a breath as he settled all the way in, and instead of moving, he lay against me.

"Last night," he began, and I silenced him, fingers pressed to his mouth.

I did not wish him to speak ill of last night. I did not wish for him to regret it.

Last night was our beginning, and I did not wish to look at it with anything less than fondness, magic fueling our passion or not.

When I was sure he would be silent, I drew away. We stared at each other for a moment longer before Casamir's lips fell to mine and he began to move. I moaned at the feel of him inside me, and his tongue dipped into my mouth, twisting with my own. He still tasted like me, and a powerful and warm feeling blossomed in my chest. I opened wider for him, lifted my hips higher to meet his thrusts.

Casamir pulled back, bracing his arms on either side of my head, and watched me with an intensity that made me feel raw and exposed, as though he could see my heart and how it beat hard for him.

He shifted to reach for my leg, which he cradled

in the crook of his arm. A sound escaped my mouth at the pleasure of this new position, and I pressed my head into my pillow as wave after wave of pleasure rocked my body. Casamir bent to kiss my neck and take the skin into his mouth, sucking hard.

I moaned, my fingers tangling in his hair, bracing behind his neck.

"Yes," I whispered. "More."

"More of what, sweet creature?" he asked.

I did not know, to be truthful, but I lifted my other leg and dug my heel into his ass, and my body moved against his, driving apart and ramming together, and there was nothing beyond this to focus on or to feel.

I pressed my palms against the headboard to keep my head from hitting it. Casamir seemed to notice because he placed his hands atop my head, and then he kissed me, moving harder, faster, deeper. Our bodies became damp and the air smelled thick with our sex, each of us on the cusp of erupting.

I felt my release in my bones and Casamir followed after, his arms shaking as he lowered himself to kiss me, his tongue stroking my mouth with a soft passion I felt deep in my gut. When he pulled away, I questioned who this man was who had made love to me so tenderly.

It left me feeling strange—changed.

There was a part of me that wanted to run from it, but I was still beneath Casamir and he had yet to leave my body. I could not deny that I liked it here.

He brushed my lips with the tip of his finger.

"Are you okay?" he asked, his voice a quiet whisper.

"Yes," I said, though my body still shook. "More than."

He offered a ghost of a smile, as if he did not trust my words.

"Are you okay?" I asked in return.

He smiled a little more.

"Yes," he said. "More than."

He bent to kiss me, and I closed my eyes, expecting to feel his mouth on mine, but instead, he pressed his lips to my forehead and rolled off. I instantly felt cold without him and wanted to turn into his heat, but he left the bed entirely, stepping outside the curtains.

I considered asking him what he was doing, but I could hear water dripping into a basin and could guess. He returned only a few seconds later with a cloth in hand. He said nothing as he handed it to me and closed the curtains as I cleaned myself—first focusing on the blood that had since dried on my hands from the ax, then the rest.

"I'm...finished," I said, feeling awkward when Casamir appeared and held out his hand to take the cloth. I hesitated.

"We have become too familiar with one another for this to be embarrassing."

He might be right, but that did not keep the warmth from my cheeks as I handed over the cloth.

When he returned, he placed one knee on the bed but did not return to my side.

"Do you wish to leave?" he asked, his expression neutral, though I sensed that he was working hard to remain in control of his emotions, unwilling to show disappointment if I said yes. But I had no intention of leaving. I was still cold, and I wanted his warmth.

"No," I whispered.

Casamir released a breath and then pulled the blankets back so we could crawl beneath them. I waited for him to lie down before I rested beside him, curling against his warmth. I let my hand rest on his chest, and beneath my palm, I could feel his heart beating fast. I closed my eyes, and in the quiet, the steady thrum lulled me into a quiet sense of calm. But as my body relaxed, Casamir spoke.

"What happened to your family?" he asked.

I opened my eyes and stared into the dark. It was a question that made my heart clench, as if he had taken it into his hand and squeezed.

"They died," I said.

Thinking about it made me sick and sad. I was the reason they were gone, the reason I was alone. My blood had killed my mother, I had wished for my sister's death, and my father had died of heartbreak from her loss.

"Your sister died too? Or was she murdered?"

I curled my fingers on his chest, and he covered it with his.

"Tell me," he said. "Please."

It took me a moment to speak because I suddenly felt like my tongue was swollen.

"When I was younger, I would dance with the fairies on the edge of the forest. Small ones with butterfly wings. I loved them and they never harmed me. When my sister found out, she chased them away. I was so angry, I wished she were dead, and she transformed into a deer right before my eyes and raced into the forest."

I paused and swallowed the thickness in my throat.

"I searched for her in the forest for years, and on the final day of the seventh year, I found her, resting beneath a tree, but when I started to go to her, an arrow flew from the trees and hit her.

I will never forget how her eyes widened, and as she fell, she became human again. There was so much blood, and I couldn't stop it, so I just held her and told her how sorry I was...how much I wished I could undo what I had done. Then, as if the forest had not punished us enough, I noticed something slithering and saw that roots were shifting beneath us, wrapping around my sister. I screamed and clawed at the wood, but the tree took her."

This time, I could not keep the tears from sliding down my cheeks. I took a shuddering breath and whispered, "I have never wished for anything since."

There was a beat of silence as Casamir's hands tightened around me.

"Your sister is not dead," he said.

I pushed away from him and sat up. "Do *not*."

Casamir rose with me and reached for my hands. I tried to pull away, but he kept them close to his chest.

"She is healing, not dead," he said quickly. "*Trust me*."

I stared at him, searching his eyes for the truth, but he looked so serious and so sincere, it took the breath out of me.

"What are you saying?"

"If the tree took her as you said, then she is healing. It is not quick. She could be within its roots for years, a hundred even, but it is likely that her heart still beats."

I scrambled from the bed.

"*Creature*," Casamir hissed. "Where are you going?"

"To my sister!" I said, searching for my clothes, but recalling I had come only in a robe, I ran for the door.

Casamir caught me about the waist.

"It is too dangerous tonight."

"Let me go!" I snapped, clawing at his hands, but he would not let me go.

"Not in the dark," he said, his mouth against my ear. "Please, sweet creature."

"But she is *alive!*" My voice broke. I was no longer alone.

"And she is likely still in the tree, where she will be tomorrow."

His words stole my fight, and I sagged against him. His arms were tight around me, and his head still rested in the crook of my neck.

"I will take you tomorrow. I will take you as soon as day breaks. I promise. I swear it."

After a moment, I turned to face him.

"Why promise?" I asked. "Why swear?"

He seemed confused. "Because…it is what you want."

My chest felt warm and open, and I felt as if my heart were beating in my whole body. I gripped his face and pulled him to me. As our lips collided, we staggered and Casamir's hands fell to my ass, gripping me tight, his arousal hard between us.

"Down," I commanded, and we knelt to the floor. I guided him to his back and straddled him, grinding over his cock. I bent to kiss him again, letting my tongue collide with his. Casamir's fingers pressed into me as I chased friction we both sought, and when that wasn't enough, I guided him inside me, hips grinding into hips, hands planted against his chest. When I grew too tired, he sat up and gripped me, helping me move, our foreheads resting together, our bodies warm and wet. As the pressure built between us, Casamir kissed me, lavishing my mouth with his tongue, and I came, collapsing against him. He held me as he settled onto his back, and we lay there until our breaths evened.

"N."

I winced at the letter, and Casamir stiffened, expecting me to tear away from him. But instead, I remained where I was, body heavy against his.

"I did not mean it," I said.

"You did," he said. "At least when you first spoke the words, but I did not offer it because of the bargain. Think of it as a gift, another letter closer to freedom."

"Is that what you want?" I asked, feeling the slightest twinge of pain at the thought that he would want me gone.

"Isn't that what you want?" he countered.

I thought about it, uncertain now, and after a moment, I spoke.

"I want a choice. To stay or go."

Wasn't that freedom? A choice.

"Which would you choose?"

"I cannot say," I said, my words slow and sleepy. "I am not free."

Casamir stared, and I wondered what he was thinking, what was moving behind his dark eyes, but he rose to sit. With my legs wrapped around his waist and my arms around his neck, he stood and carried me to bed. As I lay beside him, my mind reeled with thoughts of what it would be like to do this for the rest of my life, and I did not hate it.

CHAPTER EIGHTEEN
The Old Willow

"Wake, sweet creature," said a voice, quiet and warm.

Groggily, I opened my eyes to find Casamir standing over me, fully dressed. A golden-orange light burned behind him. The sun was rising.

"It is daybreak," he said. "And I have promised to take you to your sister."

Those words woke me immediately, and I rose and swung my legs over the bed. I was naked and suddenly beneath Casamir's appraising gaze. His eyes roved and my skin warmed, the bottom of my stomach igniting with a desire so keen, I shifted closer to the edge and parted my legs.

Casamir's gaze held there, and his tongue slid across his bottom lip.

"Oh, sweet creature," he rasped. "This morning is not for temptation, for I have made promises."

He touched my chin and tipped my head back while his other hand fisted my hair and he ravaged my mouth.

He pulled away with a groan and rested his forehead against mine.

"Get dressed," he said, stepping back to hand me a pile of clothes.

I was surprised when he did not watch and instead crossed the room toward his plants as I changed into a pair of leggings and a long dress with high slits for riding.

"Rested?" a voice asked.

I snapped my head toward the mirror, and my mouth fell open, but I could not respond. I had forgotten about him.

"I—"

"Ignore him," said Casamir, his back still to me.

"How do you ignore him?" I asked. "He's *there*."

He had *seen* everything. *Heard* everything.

My cheeks flushed at the thought.

"Trust me, the more he speaks, the easier it is."

"Do not worry, creature," the mirror said. "I am used to the prince's lovemaking."

"Oh really?" I asked, my embarrassment overtaken by a sudden shock of jealousy.

"Do not say it like that, you foolish thing," Casamir said.

"How should he say it then?" I asked.

"Yes, how should I say it?" the mirror echoed.

Casamir continued to inspect his plants, oblivious to the anger boiling my blood.

"To say I have made love to anyone but you is a fallacy," he said. "And I have spent the better part of ten years pleasuring only myself. If the mirror has been watching anyone fuck, it must be one of my brothers."

"Would he not know the difference?" I countered.

"Well, he is only a mirror," he said, and then he turned to me, his expression serious, growing far more severe the longer he stared. After a second, he crossed to me and reached for the remaining piece of clothing that lay on the bed—a cloak that he draped around my shoulders and clasped at the front. He let his fingers glide down the edges of each side until his fingers twined with mine.

"Beautiful," he said.

My gaze fell to his lips, and I leaned closer, just grazing his mouth with my own when the mirror spoke.

"That was well done, Prince," he said.

We both glared.

"You know you do not *have* to speak," Casamir said.

"I only wish to offer a compliment," the mirror said. "You have improved since last time."

My brows lowered, and before I could speak, Casamir took my hand and dragged me to the door.

"It is time to go."

He did not let go of my hand until we came to the courtyard where a white horse grazed. His coat shined beneath the sun, so bright it was almost blinding.

"I did not know you had horses," I said. I had seen no stables since I had arrived.

"I don't," he said. "Balthazar is wild, but he has agreed to help us today."

"You do not keep animals, but you keep humans?"

"Animals are pure of heart," he said. "Humans are not."

I did not disagree. I pet Balthazar's nose.

"Have you ridden before?" he asked.

"Of course," I said, and he stepped back as I mounted

Balthazar. He followed and settled behind me, arms circling my waist, hands smoothing down my arms to my hands.

"Do you know the way?" he asked.

"I know the tree. I go there every day," I said, then corrected myself. "I used to. It is an old willow by the wide river."

"Hold on," he said. Our fingers tightened into Balthazar's mane, and the horse bolted into the Enchanted Forest. I could not tell if Casamir guided the steed or if he knew the way, but he carried us deeper into the woods on a smooth and even gait, dodging limbs and bramble walls. Soon we came to a river, which Balthazar followed until it forked, at which point he made a hard left, right into the river.

The water splashed us, and I gasped at how frigid it was. Casamir chuckled near my ear but said nothing as Balthazar waded through to the bank and continued galloping through the forest, always within sight of the river, which curved like a snake around tall trees and between hills. There came a moment when the surroundings looked familiar and I realized I knew this place.

My heart rose into my throat as the willow came into view, its long, slender branches sweeping the ground like a cascading waterfall.

Balthazar slowed to a stop and Casamir dismounted. I followed, and once my feet touched the ground, I raced to the tree. The ground was disturbed by an elaborate root system, making it difficult to stand beneath its eaves, and yet I managed to walk the perimeter until I found the spot where Winter had once lain. But there was no sign that anyone had risen from these roots.

I felt panicked as I fell to the ground and tried to pry the roots apart, but they would not give.

Then Casamir's hands covered mine and I stilled, meeting his dark gaze.

"Feel her," he said and pressed my palms flat to the roots.

"I *can't*," I said, my voice too high, my head too light.

"Breathe, sweet creature," he said. "Your sister is not far away."

My chest rose and fell rapidly for a few seconds longer before I closed my eyes and took a deep breath, focusing on the warmth of Casamir's hands atop mine and the roughness of the willow's roots beneath my palms.

Then I felt it—a faint pulse against my skin.

A heartbeat.

I opened my eyes.

"She's *alive*."

I met Casamir's gaze, and I could not quite place the expression on his face. It was caught somewhere between kind and compassionate, and I was not prepared for how it would complement his beauty.

"I told you," he said.

My brows lowered. "But...how long until she's healed? It has been ten years."

"The willow does not often heal mortals," he said. "She likely only did because each of you have some fae blood."

For the first time in my life, I was grateful for that little bit of blood.

"She may rise in a day or ten. She may rise long after you and I are dead and the world no longer looks the same."

Tears welled in my eyes at the thought of being without her for any length of time beyond today, now that I knew her heart beat.

"How will I know? She cannot rise alone."

"She will not be alone," said Casamir. "The fae will help her. By then, she will be fully one of them...one of us."

My gaze snapped to him, but he did not look at me, as if he did not wish to know my reaction to this news.

He rose abruptly and left me beneath the willow.

I lingered a moment longer and pressed a kiss to the willow roots, whispering, "I love you. I'll come for you. I *promise*."

When I left the eaves of the tree, Casamir stood at the center of the meadow, Balthazar waiting nearby. To an untrained eye, he looked menacing and dangerous, but I knew the truth.

I started toward him but stopped a few feet short of reaching him.

"Why did you do this for me?" I asked.

"Because it was what you wanted," he answered.

I shifted on my feet, swallowing hard.

"And what do you want?"

I thought he would reply quickly, but he waited a moment, and when he answered, he spoke slowly, almost uncertain. "I would like to keep my name."

"Why is your name so important?"

"It reminds me of who I was and who I have become," he said.

"And you cannot remember all that if you choose a new one?"

He nearly flinched, and I wondered what tumbled around inside his head as I spoke. I stepped closer, careful, as if I were approaching a predator. I stopped inches from him, our heads inclined, the tension between us thickening, a weight I could barely breathe beneath.

"Is it the name you truly want?" I whispered, my eyes lowered to his lips.

"There is nothing else to desire beyond a true name," he said. "Yours or mine."

His words confused me. "Not even love?"

Casamir's brows lowered. "Are you taunting me?"

"No," I said.

He stared at me and then let his finger trail softly over my cheek, warming my skin.

"Could you love me?" he whispered.

The question stole my breath and burned my lungs in the silence that followed.

I wanted to answer, to whisper yes into the space between us, but I was afraid.

What if I confessed but he could not love me in return?

Did it even matter if I was content to spend my days with him?

His features grew cold and distant, and he took a step back. The tension that had built around us burst, leaving my limbs weak.

"We should return," he said and crossed to Balthazar.

He waited for me to mount before joining me, and he rode without holding me or the horse. And while I would usually be hyperaware of his presence, I was now hyperaware of his absence and found that I hated it far more than I had ever hated the Prince of Thorns.

CHAPTER NINETEEN

What is Love?

Could you love me?

What a *stupid* question, I seethed as we returned to the castle. Of course the creature never could, never would love me.

Despite being desperate to touch her, I curled my fingers into fists, refusing. I could not let myself fall deeper into this well—into the hope that she might find me somehow enough.

I thought I would feel some sort of relief when the castle came into view, but I would find no such reprieve. Instead, this feeling of distance created turmoil in my chest.

Balthazar halted, and I dismounted, only to turn and help my creature dismount, my hands closing around her waist.

Once she was safely on the ground, she turned to me.

"G," she said.

My brows lowered. "What?"

"A letter from my name," she said, and then her eyes fell from mine as she added, "You will never know how grateful I am to know my sister lives."

Without another word, she whirled and left the garden. I stared after her, even when I could no longer see her, my mind a chaotic mix of emotions I did not understand, and the longer I felt them—the confusion and strange affection for this mortal woman—the more frustrated I grew. And so I found myself again outside the mortal prince's cell.

"What is love?" I demanded.

I was not certain what he had been doing before I arrived, but he had his face pressed between the bars of his small window so hard that when he turned to me, I could see their impression on his face.

His eyes widened. "Wh-what?"

"Love," I said. "What is it? What does it *feel* like?"

His mouth opened and closed, and then he cleared his throat.

"Well, it is a feeling," he answered. "It...uh...it feels *nice*."

"Nice?" I repeated with a click of my tongue.

"Yes, you know...*good*," he said, rubbing his palms on his clothes as if he were sweating profusely, though it was cool in his cell. "It's good."

I drew my bottom lip between my teeth, nodding.

"Tell me your greatest desire," I said.

He stared. "Is this a trick?"

"It is not," I said, and when the prince did not speak, I added, "You have my word."

Though that promise felt like glass between my teeth.

"My greatest desire is not so simple," he said. "While

183

it is to be free, if I do not return to my kingdom with a golden apple from a tree that grows in the depths of the Glass Mountains, I cannot marry my beloved."

It was the most articulate he had been since I began seeking his help.

I raised a brow. "Must you marry her?"

The prince balked. "Of course! If I do not marry her, she will marry someone else."

"Then she must not love you."

"She loves me," he said. "But she is a princess, and all princesses must marry."

"Who says?"

The prince hesitated and then answered, "Her father."

"And if her father is dead?"

"If he is dead and no one has married the princess, then there is no king."

"So you wish to be king?" I asked.

The prince said nothing, and I knew I had hit at the root of his desire.

"So all this advice you have offered…?"

"I did not lie," said the prince defensively. "You asked how to make a maiden fall in love with you, not how to fall in love with *her*."

My face felt hot with frustration, but the prince was not wrong.

"So…has she fallen for you yet?" he asked.

"Would you be here if she had?"

The prince paled, but he was not deterred. "But you have fallen for her?"

"That is what I am trying to figure out," I gritted out.

"Well, how do you feel?" he asked.

"Insane," I said.

"I think you were insane before her," said the prince. I glared.

"I cannot describe it," I said after a moment. "I only know that I do not wish to know the world without her."

The prince hummed softly and then replied, "Well, if you are not in love, then that is a promising start."

I met his gaze and scowled. "You are most unhelpful."

I vanished, returning to my room. Naeve, who had been making my bed, yelped as I landed on the mattress. I ignored her, reached for a pillow, covered my face, and screamed.

"Feeling better?" the mirror asked when I was finished.

"No," I said, the pillow muffling my snappy response.

Naeve yanked it off my face and then hit me with it. I scowled at her, and she hit me again.

"Why are you here? You should be wooing your creature! You have only three days to make her love you!"

"I have done all I could!" I said, sitting up.

"You mean you have fucked her?" asked Naeve.

"I did more than fuck, you naughty little sprite!"

"And you think that is enough?"

"I cannot *make* her love me, you idiot! Love is a choice, and she has not chosen me."

There was silence, and then I heard Naeve's sharp inhale.

"Well, we have finally made progress."

I stared at her, confused.

"What are you talking about?"

"If love is a choice, then you can choose it too," she said.

"She is supposed to fall in love with me, Naeve, or have you forgotten?"

She shook her head. "You have one day to live however you desire before you forget yourself forever. How do you wish to spend it?"

I was silent.

"How?" she demanded.

I growled, my teeth clenched together as I answered, "With her, you frustrating thing! I would spend it with her!"

As those words left me, I suddenly felt exhausted.

"She makes me feel like it won't matter if I have a name or not. So long as I know her, I will know myself."

A choked cry erupted in the silence, and I looked toward the mirror.

"Are you…crying?" I asked.

"Of course not," he said, voice quivering. "I am only a mirror."

I rolled my eyes.

"Perhaps instead of worrying over whether she loves you, you can spend these last few days loving her."

"What if she doesn't want it?" I asked.

"She seemed accepting from my vantage point," said the mirror.

I scowled. "Could you…*not* for once in your life?"

"It is not as if I have a choice. I am only…"

"If you say 'only a mirror' one more time," I warned, the words slipping through my teeth.

"Focus!" Naeve snapped. She lifted her hand as if she were going to slap me, and I bared my teeth. "Don't let this woman forget you, Casamir, even when you do not know your name."

I looked at her and then at my hands. "What should I do then?"

"May I once again suggest a picnic," said the mirror.

CHAPTER TWENTY
A Pleasant Picnic

U, I, A, S, N.

I lay on my bed, staring at the ceiling again, considering how the letters of Casamir's true name fit together and which ones I might be missing, I found myself wondering what would happen when I learned his name, when I spoke it and managed to free myself. Did I have to leave? Did I have to return to my lonely cottage on the edge of the Enchanted Forest? If I stayed and Casamir did not know himself, would he still know me?

The thought hurt more than I liked to admit.

Of course, all this would be remedied if I loved him.

But what was love? True, I had loved my mother, my sister, my father. I had loved them and hurt them.

I did not want my love to hurt Casamir, not when he took away so much of my pain.

A knock sounded at my door, and I let out a breath, blinking rapidly to clear my eyes, which had blurred with tears.

I sat up and stared at the door, mistrusting who might be on the other side.

The knock sounded again, and I rolled onto my knees and reached for my ax, which had been returned to my bedside table, likely by Naeve. Its handle was no longer riddled with thorns but smooth—Casamir's magic, if I had to guess.

"Come in," I said.

The door opened, and Casamir entered.

I was startled to see him, given his cold departure, but as he closed the door, a slow smile spread across his face.

"Preparing for battle, creature?" he asked.

I held the ax to my chest.

"That depends," I said. "Have you come to declare war?"

"I was thinking something a little less bloody."

I raised a brow, and his features became a little more serious.

"Perhaps a picnic?"

I pressed my lips together, attempting not to smile at the thought of the Prince of Thorns on a pleasant picnic.

"Do you even like picnics?" I asked.

"I like anything with you," he said.

I stared and swallowed.

"Well?" he prompted.

"Yes," I said. "I'll go on a picnic with you."

He smiled, full and real, and as if he could not be any more beautiful, he suddenly was. He stole my breath.

"I will meet you in the courtyard," he said.

I nodded, and when he left my room, I let out a long breath and collapsed against the bed.

What was happening to me that I desired his presence so much? This was more than wanting his body in mine.

I had sought him out.

I had wanted him.

And lying here alone had only made me wish for him more.

I rolled off the bed and knocked on the wardrobe door.

"I need something to wear to a picnic," I said.

The door opened, and I expected the elves to toss something at me as they always did, but instead, six pairs of eyes stared back, assessing. After a brief moment, the door closed quietly. I was surprised by their discreet action and continued to be when they opened the door a few seconds later to dangle another white dress before me.

I took it and held it to my chest.

"Thank you," I said and then turned from them to slip into the airy gown. It was off the shoulder with a laced front, which I tied loosely. The fabric was nearly see-through, as the fairies were keen to craft. I slipped on a pair of flat shoes and checked the mirror. My hair was wild and wispy from our earlier ride to the willow tree, and I smoothed it into a braid before I left for the court-yard, unable to calm the strange fluttering in my stomach.

It did not lessen, even when I found Casamir waiting for me. If anything, it burned hotter, filling my veins and flushing my skin. He wore black trousers and a loose white shirt, the collar of which was open, exposing the long column of his neck and chest, his creamy skin marked by my mouth.

His eyes darkened as he took me in, and I shivered beneath his gaze.

"Are you ready, sweet creature?"

"Yes," I said, voice quiet.

He held out his hand, and as I took it, he drew me to him, his arm snaking around my waist.

"You are beautiful," he murmured.

I smiled up at him. "You are getting very good at giving that compliment."

His fingers touched beneath my chin. "It is easy to say when it is the truth."

I felt as though I couldn't breathe and let my gaze fall to his chest, fingers tracing his skin.

"I thought we were going on a picnic," I said.

"We are."

"You have no basket," I said. "No blanket."

He chuckled, and the sound drew my attention again. His eyes gleamed with mirth, and I loved it. I wanted to see that expression in his face every day.

"Come, sweet creature."

Casamir did not release my hand as he led me into his garden. As we passed clusters of blooming flowers, sprites rose from the petals, flying in swarms ahead of us. As before, the garden grew thicker and fuller the farther we walked, and despite being with Casamir, I could not help feeling on edge. The garden seemed to open up and fall away until we stood at the center of a clearing where the ground was covered in small white flowers. Trees with crooked and twisting trunks framed the space, but it was beneath the tallest one that our picnic was splayed on a white quilt. Amid bouquets of small, pink flowers and pillar candles were bottles of wine, plates of meat and cheese, and sweet treats.

"Is it to your liking?" he asked.

"More than," I said, smiling.

I had never seen a more beautiful picnic, but then I had never been on one.

He held my hand until we were seated and poured wine into elegant glasses. I watched as Casamir reclined on the blanket, looking relaxed and far too beautiful. I sipped my wine, which tasted like raspberries, both sweet and tart. Now that we were here, I felt so uncertain and so confused.

"I never thought any part of the Enchanted Forest could be beautiful," I said.

"It is all beautiful," he said. "But that does not make it any less dangerous."

I offered a small, almost sad smile. "If I didn't know better, I would think you were talking about yourself."

"You think I am beautiful?" he asked, amused.

"Of course," I said.

His stare captured and held mine, too intense to release.

I took a breath. "What are we doing?"

"Having a picnic," he said.

"No, Casamir. What are *we* doing? I don't understand this...*us*."

He frowned and then rose, setting his glass aside. He leaned toward me and drew my hair behind my ear, fingers lingering along my jaw.

"Do you need to?" he asked.

"I think I should," I said. "Before I make a mistake."

"What mistake could you possibly make?"

His mouth hovered over mine, his breath caressing my lips as he waited for my reply, but it never came. Instead, I let my tongue slip into his mouth and gave in to his kiss, which deepened with a slow caress.

Casamir tugged on the ties of my dress, and I helped him pull the neckline down, slipping my arms from the sleeves. It pooled around my waist. Bared to him, I swung my leg over his and he jerked me forward, hands beneath my knees, until I settled against his arousal. I groaned at how he fit against me. Just the promise that he would soon be inside me was pleasure, and for a brief moment, I considered how I had ever lived without this—without him.

Casamir kissed me as he squeezed my breasts and then took each one into his mouth. I gasped, raking my fingers through his hair, pulling on his long strands until he released me and brought his mouth to mine.

"Tell me what part of this is a mistake," he said, and his hands swept beneath my dress, over my thighs and hips before he gripped my ass, his fingers digging into me as he moved me against him, his arousal creating a delicious friction between my thighs. All the while, Casamir's mouth explored my jaw and neck, my collarbone and my breasts. He was everywhere all at once, and somehow I still wanted more. Then he shifted and rolled me onto my back. He gave me no time to adjust as he moved down my body, leaving a path of fire in his wake as he descended to the apex of my thighs and kissed there, his mouth closing over my clit, his tongue dancing in gentle circles, his fingers parting my flesh, curling inside me. When I came and lay boneless and breathless, Casamir pulled my dress off and then stripped himself of his clothes. Everything inside me felt like liquid fire as I watched him, lean and hard, return to me.

He settled between my legs. I expected him to kiss me, but all he did was stare, his heavy arousal growing harder, pressing into the bottom of my stomach.

"What's wrong?" I asked.

"Nothing," he said. "I am just trying to memorize you."

"Are you saying you will forget me?" I asked, my tone light, teasing, but he frowned and I felt the dread blossoming inside me.

"I don't know."

I studied him and then took his face between my hands.

"I wish that I could have at least given you freedom," he said. "I do not wish for you to watch me fade away." There was something in his dark and deep eyes I had never seen before—a hint of fear—and it felt like it was more for me than for him.

My heart stuttered in my chest.

"You won't," I swore. "I will remind you of who you are."

"Every day?" he asked.

"Until you remember."

"I will never remember."

"Will you remember me?" I asked, voice trembling slightly, unable to keep my fear at bay.

"I never wish to forget you."

We stared at each other in silence for a moment, and then I brought him to me and kissed him, reaching between us to position him against my heat. In one thrust, he was inside me.

There was a slow and sweet rhythm to the way we began. I felt every ridge of him as he moved, and our breaths came quietly, quickening as his pace increased. I began to move with him, and then we were suddenly completely different and desperate.

His hand went to my neck, but he did not squeeze. I waited, and then ordered it. He kissed me instead, and when he broke away, I felt his fingers press on either side of my neck and relished in the pressure building in my head. When he released me, the pleasure nearly shattered me.

I gave a guttural cry and lifted my head toward his. Our lips crashed in a messy kiss as I gripped his forearms for some semblance of control. But I was already lost, and when I came, he followed shortly after, my muscles clenching around him, eager for every drop of come he possessed.

We lay on the quilt afterward, and Casamir fed me grapes and plums. They were sweet and ripe, and after I finished, he would kiss me, tongue swirling, lapping at the sugar on my skin.

There came a point when he hooked my leg over his and spread me wide and entered me as he lay on his side behind me. I arched against him, my hand anchoring behind his head so I could bring his mouth to mine until I could hold on no longer and instead braced myself against the ground as he thrust inside me. My eyes watered from the bliss of it, and he kept going until I felt like I could no longer handle the ecstasy of it and I burst open.

As I came down from the high, I felt raw and exposed, and I wondered if Casamir could see how I felt—how much I *wished* to have this for the rest of my life.

He placed a kiss in the hollow of my neck and spoke near my ear.

"I would give you a letter," he said. "But I fear I cannot recall my name."

I frowned and lifted my head to look at him. "It isn't time to forget."

He smiled faintly.

"Perhaps I have miscounted the days," he said in a sleepy voice, and as he fell into an untroubled sleep, I lay awake, desperate for his name.

CHAPTER TWENTY-ONE
The Riddle

We left the clearing and returned to the castle where I followed Casamir to his room. For a few more hours, I was able to forget my fear of losing him. When he was in front of me, touching me, making love to me, it was hard to imagine he would ever forget me, but I knew the evil of magic. It had hurt me before and it would again.

Casamir slept beside me, his warmth a welcome weight, and though I was exhausted, I could not stop my mind from reeling, turning over the mirror's riddle in an attempt to make sense of the words.

His name knows no stranger.
It is the wail on the lips of a birthing mother,
the howl from the mouth of a grieving lover.
It is the cry that breaks the night when death is summoned
and the scream that echoes at daybreak when truth makes
you ache.
You know his name. You have felt it.

I turned my head and stared at his profile and tried

to imagine returning to my solitary life, knowing that his memory would always live beneath my skin. I would never be able to let him go. He would drive me mad, and he would not even know it because he would not know me.

Despite being tired, I left the bed and slipped into the white dress the elves had made me for the picnic. Dawn was just breaking, and a pure golden light warmed the curtains covering the windows. I crossed to the corner of the room where Casamir's plants thrived.

"Will he remember why he loved them?" I asked as I took a velvet leaf between my fingers.

"He will remember nothing about himself," said the mirror. "That is the power of losing one's name."

My chest felt tight, and I swallowed something hard in my throat.

"And if I were to give him my name?" I asked and then looked at the mirror. This time, I saw my reflection, haunted and pale.

"Well then, that would be power too."

I left Casamir to sleep and wandered into the garden, hoping to clear my head. I needed time to think, to cycle through the letters I had and the words I knew. Now that I was faced with losing Casamir, I felt a bone-deep sorrow.

It hurt and ached.

I had been alone so long, I never thought I would desire anyone, but here I was, wishing for an elven prince to love me.

I halted in my steps.

Surely that was not what I had meant.

I wanted Casamir to remember me, not *love* me.

A sudden and intense rush of dizziness overtook me, and I shook, unable to breathe as I came to terms with the truth of my feelings. I wanted Casamir to love me because I loved him, but I needed his name.

What was his *name*?

The more frustrated I grew, the less hold I had on my emotions. I felt frantic and my chest tightened, and my heart felt as though it was beating all over my body. I bent at the waist and tried to take in air, repeating the letters of Casamir's name.

U, I, A, S, N.

I said them over and over until I could breathe again.

Slowly, my thoughts turned to the mirror's riddle, and I recalled the times when I had wailed and howled and cried at my family's deaths. My grief had spanned mornings, and all I had ever felt was agony. All I had felt was—

Anguish.

My heart rose. That had to be Casamir's true name.

My body danced with delight, vibrating with excitement. I whirled, intending to race to him and speak it against his lips as I confessed my love, but as I turned, I came face-to-face with a man.

"Well, hello," he said, and while he tried to sound pleasant, I immediately felt on edge.

I got the sense by the way he approached, as if I were a wild animal, hands outstretched, palms flat, that he had been trying to sneak up on me.

He wore a purple hat and strange purple clothes that seemed to be missing buttons down the front, for his shirt hung open, exposing his chest and stomach.

"Who are you?" I asked, my pulse racing. He tried to

circle me, but I followed, wishing I had my ax. I would show him what to fear then.

"I am a prince. A mortal one," he added, as if I could not tell. No fae would wear such clothing. No fae would approach me as if I were the threat. "My name is Flynn."

He paused to bow and added, "At your service."

"I do not need your service," I said.

He watched me, blue eyes sparkling.

"Are you the maiden the prince is in love with?"

I wanted to ask how he knew about me, but I was stunned by his words.

Had he said the prince was in love with me?

I opened my mouth and then closed it, finally deciding to ask, "Why are you here?"

"The same reason you are here, I imagine. We are captives, are we not?"

I did not speak and instead took a step away.

"Do not be afraid," he said, inching closer. "I will not hurt you. I am here to rescue you."

"I do not need rescuing," I said.

"It looks to me like you do," he said.

Casamir's name was poised on my tongue. I knew if I called, he would come, but before I could speak, something tight wrapped around my wrists and mouth—vines.

Something struck me from behind, and I fell to my knees. When I looked up, a cluster of pixies flew from behind me, hovering near Prince Flynn. They were the ones who had left slugs in my room on my first night in Casamir's castle.

Each held out a hand, and he popped a button from the cuff of his sleeves. The pixies took them in hand, the buttons as big as them, and they dragged them away, wings beating furiously.

It was their magic that restrained me, their magic he had bargained for. Two remained, each sitting on one of his shoulders.

"The pixies tell me you have been to the Glass Mountains."

Fucking fae. Casamir would not have the pleasure of tearing them to pieces because I would tear them limb from limb.

"You will take me there," he said. "And once I have obtained a golden apple from the Mountains, you will come to my kingdom and aid me in conquering the Prince of Thorns. Do you understand?"

I glared, and then he produced my ax from behind his back. and my eyes widened. Another bargain made with the pixies, no doubt.

"If you try anything, I will not hesitate to bury this blade in your head. It's what you deserve, after all, for fucking a fae prince. Up!"

I rose to my feet on shaking legs, and the mortal prince put his hand on my forearm.

"The pixies say there is a pond you depart from, and from there you call a wolf."

I tried not to react to what the pixies had told the mortal, knowing he had to have made a desperate bargain. What had the prince given up for this aid? More than buttons, I imagined.

"I shall know if you lead me astray," said the prince as he pushed me ahead. "Walk."

I led the way as I considered my next move. It was as if the pixies knew I was considering my escape, because the vines tightened on my wrists and around my mouth, but they could not stop my thoughts, which wished for Casamir, for Anguish, for my elven prince to wake and realize I was gone.

All the while, Prince Flynn kept busy, rattling away about his time in the dungeons of Casamir's palace.

"And did you know he came to me for love advice?" he was saying. "And each time he took something from me. First my hair, and then the feather in my hat, as if the hair could not grow back, as if I could not obtain another feather. The fae, they are foolish!"

His words made me cringe. Even if he managed to obtain a golden apple from the Glass Mountains, I knew he would come to regret those words, though I wondered why Casamir had asked for his hair and the feather in his hat. I knew the Prince of Thorns, and he did not ask for anything without reason.

"For a harlot, you are a picky thing."

I jerked in his hold at his horrible words, and he wrenched me against him, placing the sharp blade of my ax against my neck.

"Ah, ah, ah," he said. "Remember what I said?"

"Fuck you," I tried to say, but the vines tightened to the point that my jaw ached.

The mortal prince laughed and then pushed me forward.

"Do as you're told, and the pixies might let you survive this."

The walk to the selkie's pond seemed to take forever, but when we arrived, I turned to face the prince.

"Well? What now?" he asked.

I stayed silent. It was not as if I could speak with the

vines wrapped so tight around my mouth. He seemed to realize this and chuckled.

"Oh, of course," he said and lifted the ax. "Allow me to help."

When I started to move away, his hand braced my head.

"Careful," he whispered. "I wouldn't want to cut you."

He touched the blade of the ax to the vine and pressed. They snapped, and I felt the distinct burn of a cut on my skin.

I hissed and the prince chuckled.

"I told you not to move."

I considered kneeing him in the groin, but he still had the ax aimed at my chest, and without my hands free to grab it, I worried it would end up buried inside me.

"Now what, harlot?" he asked.

I ground my teeth.

"Drink the water," I said. "And I'll call for Wolf."

"Drink the water?"

"You must drink the water to grow small enough to ride Wolf," I said. "Do you want your apple or not?"

He looked from one shoulder to the other where the pixies still sat, and once they had confirmed what I said, Prince Flynn grabbed me and directed me to the water. He kicked my feet out from under me, and I fell hard, mud splattering my entire body.

"You drink," he commanded. "And then I will."

I could not wait to gouge out his eyes, and I would do it with my thumbs and revel in the feel of it beneath my nails. I bent, hand still tied behind my back, and slurped the muddy water into my mouth. As I did, I felt the familiar dizziness that came with growing small. I ended up in a pool of water my knee had created on the bank of the pond and waded from it onto the soft ground.

"Well, would you look at that," he said, and I watched as he hurriedly scooped water into his cupped hands and drank.

When I called Wolf, I shouted his name and hoped that the wind would carry my summons to the castle as well, but the longer we waited, the more anxious I became. Would Casamir catch up with us soon? Would he realize I was gone and think I ran away? Would he even remember me if he truly had miscounted the days?

I chewed the inside of my cheek.

"You had better not be lying," the prince threatened as a shadow passed over our heads.

When I looked up, Wolf was circling.

"What is that?" the prince demanded.

"Wolf," I said.

"That is not a wolf!"

"I did not say Wolf was a wolf," I replied.

The raven landed and bowed his head.

"Lady Thing," he said. His beady eyes narrowed at me, noticing that my hands were tied behind my back and blood dripped down my face from the slice of my ax. "How may I assist?"

"This is Prince Flynn of the Kingdom of…" I paused and looked at the prince. I did not know from where he came, but I wanted to know, because later, when I had plucked his eyes from his head, I would return them to his father in a glass coffin, so that his whole kingdom would know what happened when he crossed me.

Prince Flynn hesitated and then spoke. "The Kingdom of Rook."

"Rook," I repeated. "He wishes to be taken to the Glass Mountains to obtain a golden apple."

"She must go too," Flynn added quickly. "You must take us both."

The raven looked from the prince to me.

"Of course," he said. "But, Lady Thing, you cannot ride with your hands tied. Allow me."

The prince raised the ax to threaten Wolf, but he moved quickly and snapped the vines around my wrists, then he shifted and plucked the prince up by the scruff of his neck and launched into the sky. The ax fell from his hand and landed at my feet, and I was hit hard by the violent splash of mud and water.

The mortal's arms flailed and despite how tiny he had become, I could still hear his desperate screams as the raven continued higher and higher until they were nothing more than a tiny, black dot in the sky.

"I command you to let me go!" he said, and when that did not work, he dissolved into tears. "Please, let me go! Let me go! I will give you anything, anything!"

Wolf obeyed and let the tiny prince drop, but before he could hit the ground, a large hawk shot from the trees and snatched him up, gobbling him whole.

I stood, staring blankly at the sky where he had been, before I knelt and drank from the pond, head spinning as I grew. When I came to my full height, something zoomed past my face—the two pixies who had helped the prince capture me. They came so close, I could feel the vibration of their wings and hear their shrill laughs.

I reached out and managed to capture one in my

palm, its joyful cackle turning into a terrified scream as I squeezed. The pixie cracked and burst, and when I opened my hand, its bloody and broken body lay at the center of my hand, wings contorted, legs twitching.

A high-pitched scream sounded, and I looked up in time to see the other pixie racing toward me, but before it could land a blow to my face, I slapped it, and it landed some distance away in the grass and did not rise again.

I washed my hands free of the blood and bone in the water and reached for my ax when I noticed black thorns and solid shadows trailing across the ground. As I straightened and turned, I found Casamir before me, his magic surrounding us like a wall, a comfort I never thought I would want but desired now forever.

He took me by the shoulders and brought me close, his eyes as black as the night sky, gleaming like the stars.

"Casamir," I breathed.

I wrapped my arms around him, though he looked vicious and bloody. If I had to guess, the other pixies who had helped the prince capture me had met their ends at his hands.

"You are hurt," he said.

"It is only a scratch," I said, pulling back to look at him. "The prince is dead."

Casamir bared his teeth.

"I am sorry. I did not know—" he began.

"It's all right, Casamir," I said and pressed my fingers to his lips. "It does not matter. I am well and I know your name. Your true name."

The harshness etched on his face did not ease.

"My name?"

My brows lowered. "Aren't you pleased?"

I thought he would be. Wasn't this what he wanted?

It was what he had said when I'd asked him what he wanted most.

My name. My true name.

"I lied," he said. "When you asked what I wanted most. I want you. I know myself when I am with you."

"Casamir," I said and drew a stray piece of his hair behind his ear, then I smiled before whispering, "My name is Gesela."

His eyes widened, and I leaned in, whispering his name before my mouth met his.

CHAPTER TWENTY-TWO

Happily Ever After

It was almost noon, and the sun burned high in the sky as I road into the town of Elk on Balthazar's back, dressed in a gown of thorn and shadow. On my head, I wore a crown of twigs and iridescent wings, a gift from Casamir. They'd come from the backs of the pixies who had aided the mortal prince in abducting me. I wore it proudly, a mark of my status as his future wife.

The thought made my chest feel warm, and as it spread through my limbs, I sat up taller.

"Gesela," Casamir had murmured as we lay together in bed once we returned home from the selkie's pond, once we had washed ourselves of the mud and blood. "Princess of the Kingdom of Thorn."

I shivered at the sound of my name on his lips, at the title he would bestow on me.

I looked down at him, tracing his mouth. "But that is my true name," I said. "Only you can call me by my true name."

Only he and death.

He smiled. "True," he said. "What would you like to be called by everyone else?"

My grin matched his. "Princess would suffice," I said, pausing. "Princess...Ella. It is what my sister would call me."

I only hoped that one day soon, she would emerge from the roots of the willow tree where she had lain and healed to hear her call me that again.

"Princess Ella it is," Casamir said.

I laughed quietly, shaking my head.

Casamir raised a brow. "What is it?"

"The selkie was right," I said. "And so was Wolf. They both said I would come to rule at your side."

The elven prince did not speak. He only stared, and I bent, my lips close to his.

"How does one turn a raven into a wolf?" I asked.

"Hmm," he said, his arms tightening around me. "I suppose you could make a wish and I could grant it."

"Wishes come with great consequences," I replied.

"And if the consequence means remaining at my side for the rest of our eternal life?"

"That is not a consequence," I said. "That is a gift."

We kissed and descended into our own heated madness.

Later I would ask, "Why did you demand the hair upon the prince's head and the feather in his hat?"

"The prince was too blind to see what he had before him—his golden curls might have become golden apples, his red feather a key to his cell, the buttons he traded to the pixies, feed to summon a horse. He had all the tools he needed to escape me, but he chose to use them incorrectly."

We spent the rest of the evening together in bed, and the next morning, Casamir granted my wish, which saw

Wolf the raven return to his true form as a great, white wolf.

In his true form, Wolf bowed and spoke.

"I am in your debt, Lady Thing," he said. "I will come when you call."

And as he disappeared into the surrounding wood, I mounted Balthazar who Casamir had also summoned from the Enchanted Forest.

"Are you certain you wish to return to your village?" Casamir asked before I departed.

"It is not my village," I said. "But yes, they must know what they have done to me."

I wanted them to look upon me and fear me, to know that their actions had created something far worse than a curse.

Now, as I passed cottages and shops, I smiled. The townspeople left their cottages to watch, and I heard their whispers.

I thought she was dead.

She has been ravished by fae.

Look at her dress! How indecent!

It was true the dress was indecent, exposing wide strips of skin, the thorned vines only covering my thighs and my breasts, but I loved it because it was a gift from Casamir.

I halted by the well just as bells rang in the late morning, disturbing the quiet. They were not nearly as beautiful as the ones that had drawn me into the forest, as if they were cracked, the sound harsh and jarring.

The doors to the chapel swung open, and more people spilled out onto the steps, among them many council members and the mayor of Elk, all of whom had voted to send me down the well.

In some ways, I had them to thank for my life's turn of events.

Their merrymaking silenced once they spotted me.

Behind them, Roland appeared dressed in powder blue and Elsie all in white, her straw-blond hair threaded through with white chrysanthemums.

I was not so surprised to see that the two had chosen each other. After they had led me to the well, they deserved each other.

They halted atop the steps, both pale as the snow still piled around the town.

"Gesela," Elsie said, breathless. "We—we thought you were dead."

"What a surprise it must be," I said, "to discover I am not."

Roland and Elsie exchanged a look.

"We went to your house, searched the whole thing," said Roland, who attempted a hard and indifferent expression but could not hide the haunted look in his eyes. "You were nowhere to be found."

"I imagine you did not expect to find me at all," I said. "Which must be why all my things have gone missing."

There was silence.

I looked at those gathered, their faces much the same as the day I left, a mix of pity and fear and discontent.

"What will you all do to atone?" I asked.

"Atone?" Roland seethed. "You cannot blame us for thinking you were dead! You fell down the well!"

"I can blame you all I want," I said. "There is no part of this that isn't your fault, Roland."

He shivered as I spoke his name, and I rested my

hands atop one another as I sat, elevated above them all, on Balthazar.

"I shall ask you again. How will you atone?"

The mortal ground his teeth and released Elsie's hand. Taking a step down, he drew his sword.

The gathered crowd gasped, and Elsie reached for his arm.

"No, Ro!"

I did not move as he bellowed. "You are a wicked spirit come to haunt us!"

His dramatic display brought a smirk to my lips.

"You dare draw your blade against me?"

"Do you think you are someone? Now that you have survived the wood?"

Whispers erupted, and Roland silenced them with a shout.

"Be gone, beast!" he hissed.

"She is not a beast," said Casamir's voice. "But I surely am."

The thorn and shadow of my dress began to move, sliding over my skin.

"What witchcraft is this?" Roland demanded as Casamir took form behind me, his arm banded around my breasts, hiding my nakedness now that I no longer wore his gown of thorns.

The crowd gasped in earnest now, shocked by the sight of him.

"An elven prince!" someone shouted. A few people screamed and some fainted at the sight of him, which I was certain he enjoyed.

"Silence!" Roland cried. "Gesela, what is the meaning of this?"

I felt Casamir stiffen at the sound of my name on the sheriff's lips.

"Forgive me," I said to Roland and placed a hand on Casamir's thigh to comfort him. "For I have yet to introduce you. Roland, meet my future husband, the Prince of Thorns, the seventh son, brother of the sixth, who you ordered me to kill."

"Husband?" he whispered.

A stunned silence followed.

"Yes," I said. "You asked who I was now that I had survived the forest? Here is your answer. I am Ella, lady of thorns and keeper of wings, wife of the seventh brother, and I have come to wish you only *Anguish*."

At the sound of Casamir's true name, a shattering sound filled the air, and then shards of gleaming glass rained down from the sky and speared Roland through the head, along with the mayor and every terrible townsperson who had treated me with contempt. Despite Elsie's participation, she remained unharmed, staring in horror as her new husband bled at her feet, her dress spattered with this blood.

Amid the pure clink of the glass and the screams of the villagers, I turned to my elven prince.

"I love you, Anguish of Thorn."

He pressed a hand to the side of my face, aligning our lips. "I love you, Gesela of my heart."

We kissed amid the carnage, but we did not feel the sting of the glass, for Balthazar had already begun the journey home, through the Enchanted Forest, past my sister's willow, to our castle of thorns.

And we lived happily ever after.
The End

Author's Note

Y'all know how I like my author's notes.

First, I know initially I called *Mountains Made of Glass* a *Grimm Retelling,* but it's really a fairy tale retelling as I do not just take inspiration from Grimm fairy tales. In this author's note and my references, you'll see I drew from Hans Christian Anderson and Irish fairy tales too.

I have wanted to write a fairy tale retelling for a long time because I feel like they are a great mix of fantasy and horror. They are also ridiculous and romantic. There is no explanation for any of the magic or even the curses. Things just exist in the world, and everyone in the stories accepts it.

I read a lot of fairy tales and many translations. Because of that, not everything taken from each tale is the same across stories, not even the title. I will list the translations I used at the end of this author's note, but I am also going to go into a lot of detail so maybe you can see how I use various elements of existing stories to create a new one.

First, let's talk about the title of this novella. The Glass Mountains are actually referenced in more than one fairy tale, but the details I used in MMOG came from "The Seven Ravens." The other element I took from this particular fairy tale was the use of Wolf (the raven) who flew Gesela to the mountains and the sacrifice of a limb. In "The Seven Ravens," the main character, a young girl, goes in search of her seven brothers, who were turned into ravens at her birth. To enter the mountains and find them, she must sacrifice her pinkie finger. I had Gesela sacrifice her ring finger, which seemed fitting as a reference to marriage.

The fairy tale that really started all this, however, is called "The Devil and the Three Golden Hairs." Just by the title, you probably already know where I got the idea that Gesela had to sacrifice three of Casamir's hairs to learn his true name, but what you may not know is that the start of this story comes directly from this tale. In "The Devil and the Three Golden Hairs," a man is sent on an impossible task—he must obtain three hairs from the devil's head (also, who knew the devil was a blond?). On his way, the man encounters three towns, and each one gives him a riddle or task to solve (note the use of numbers here, too, three golden hairs, three towns). In one town, the well has gone dry, and we learn it is because a toad lives under a stone at the bottom, and if it is killed, the water will return. This was the foundation of my story, and I thought, what happens if the toad is a prince? An *elven* prince (because I have always loved elves since Tolkien). What happens if all these curses that are broken have greater consequences?

The story grew from there.

In the same story, in another town, a fig tree is rotting and no longer bears fruit. We learn a mouse is gnawing at the roots. I reference this as Gesela is explaining what happens when curses are broken. Instead of figs, though, the tree bears golden fruit, which is a symbolic reference to many Grimm fairy tales (and many other myths, including Greek Mythology).

Beyond this, there are many small elements that are pulled from various stories. The first and most obvious would be most of the town names, which you can see on the map at the start of the book (Briar, Rose, Cinder), and any name given to a side character: Roland, Flynn, Elsie. These are all names used for characters in Grimm fairy tales. I also use common animals or flowers throughout the book as symbolic nods to stories, such as the goose Gesela had slaughtered at the start of the book. Geese appear often in Grimm fairy tales ("The Golden Goose," "The Goose Girl"). The idea of using numbers—seven brothers, seven letters, ten years—comes straight from a variety of Grimm retellings. Everything in these stories is either executed in a very short amount of time (like falling in love) or a ridiculous amount of time. I also use hair. You see this, of course, with Casamir's three hairs and the prince's golden curls. Many academic articles have been written about the role of hair in fairy tales, and I highly encourage you to read a few because the symbolism of hair is very interesting and at times, unexpected—particularly for me how it relates to beauty, sensuality, and sexuality.

It probably goes without saying that the idea of the true name is a reference to "Rumpelstiltskin," and at one point, Casamir warns that bargains with the fae can lead to sacrificing a newborn. The Magic Mirror is a reference to "Snow White," but so is Gesela's sister, Winter, who will eventually rise from the dead. Prince Flynn is an archetype of the typical Prince Charming who appears in all Grimm fairy tales. All this character ever does is rescue beautiful maidens from danger and then lives happily ever after, so I thought it would be hilarious to play on that, funnier when he gives terrible love advice because all he ever knows is that if you tell a woman she's pretty and save her, she has to marry you.

There are several situations in Grimm fairy tales when people are turned into animals. In "Little Brother and Little Sister," a spring speaks to the sister, informing her that if she drinks from it, she will turn into a fawn. The brother drinks instead and turns into a fawn, and through several fairy tales, witches turn various people into bears, ravens, geese, doves—the list goes on.

When Casamir tells Gesela that he will bury the selkie's head in his garden and see what grows, this is a reference to Hans Christian Anderson's "The Rose Elf," where a grieving woman places her dead lover's head in a pot and plants a jasmine bough on top. The use of the bell that leads Gesela into the woods comes from Anderson's "The Bell," which is literally a story about a bell that everyone can hear and no one can find. The ending is boring, about the glory of God, but I preferred Gesela finding her dead family instead, which is a reference to an Irish fairy tale called "The Ride with the Fairies."

The selkie did not come from a Grimm fairy tale, though they do have a story about a nixie, and I felt like if nixies existed in Grimm fairy tales, then a selkie would be just as plausible. I did not reference any particular story to bring in the selkie, but a good one to read is "The Selkie Wife," and before you ask why I didn't just choose a nixie, I'm not sure. I just felt like the sealskin worked really well as a plot device here. I also referenced two curses in the first chapter, boils and a harvest destroyed by locusts, which are biblical references. I did this because some translations of Grimm fairy tales are extremely religious and Hans Christian Anderson was *very* religious so it's a nod to the influence of Christianity.

There are several other elements I added to the story that were my own creation but I felt sounded plausible within a fairy tale world. Some include drinking from the pond and growing larger or smaller, the sealskin that sprouted from the thorn, the tears that made the flower grow and bloom with a fairy inside, the ax growing thorns, the willow healing Winter. These are just some I can think of off the top of my head.

Even given all this, there are likely more references I haven't touched on, but such is the nature of a retelling.

A final note: the Grimm Brothers are often credited with collecting existing fairy tales, while Hans Christian Anderson is noted for creating his own. I find they follow a similar tone and pattern.

I truly hope you enjoyed this tale, and before you ask, I plan on writing six more of these, one for each brother. Even the dead one.

Much love,
Scarlett

References

Andersen, Hans Christian. *Best-Loved Fairy Tales*. Illustrated by Dugald Stewart Walker and Hans Tegner. New York: Fall River Press, 2012.

Carruthers, Amelia. *Snow White and Other Examples of Jealousy Unrewarded*. Cookhill, Alcester, Warwickshire: Pook Press, 2015.

Grimm, Jacob, and Wilhelm Grimm. *The Complete Grimms' Fairy Tales*. Translated by Margaret Hunt. New Delhi: FingerPrint! Classics, 2021.

Grimm, Jacob, and Wilhelm Grimm. *Grimm's Complete Fairy Tales*. Translated by Margaret Hunt. San Diego: Canterbury Classics, 2011.

Grimm, Jacob, and Wilhelm Grimm. *The Original Folk and Fairy Tales of the Brothers Grimm: The Complete First Edition*. Translated and edited by Jack Zipes. Illustrated by Andrea Dezsö. Princeton, NJ: Princeton University Press, 2014.

A Treasury of Irish Fairy and Folk Tales. Barnes & Noble, 2016.

About the Author

USA Today bestselling author Scarlett St. Clair is a citizen of the Muscogee Nation and the author of the Hades X Persephone series, the Hades Saga, the Adrian X Isolde series, and *When Stars Come Out*.

She has a master's degree in library science and information studies and a bachelor's in English writing. She is obsessed with Greek mythology, murder mysteries, and the afterlife. For information on books, tour dates, and content, please visit scarlettstclair.com.